PARADAIS

Born in Veracruz, Mexico, in 1982, Fernanda Melchor is 'one of Mexico's most exciting new voices' (*Guardian*). Her novel *Hurricane Season* was shortlisted for the International Booker Prize, longlisted for the National Book Award, and was a *New York Times* Notable Book. *Paradais* was longlisted for the 2022 International Booker Prize.

Sophie Hughes translates Spanish and Latin American authors. She was shortlisted for the International Booker Prize in 2019 and 2020, and in 2021 she was awarded the Queen Sofía Translation Prize.

'Fernanda Melchor explores violence and inequity in this brutal novel. She does it with dazzling technical prowess, a perfect pitch for orality, and a neurosurgeon's precision for cruelty. *Paradais* is a short inexorable descent into Hell.'
— Mariana Enríquez, author of *Our Share of Night*

'Melchor evokes the stories of Flannery O'Connor, or, more recently, Marlon James's *A Brief History of Seven Killings*. Impressive.'
— Julian Lucas, *New York Times*

'Fernanda Melchor has a powerful voice, and by powerful I mean unsparing, devastating, the voice of someone who writes with rage and has the skill to pull it off.'
— Samanta Schweblin, author of *Fever Dream*

'Melchor's long, fevered sentences – which carry off daredevil moves, such as shifting tense and viewpoint from one clause to the next – combine with the emotional and physical violence of the story to produce a cacophonous effect. But time spent with her writing leaves no doubt: the unholy noise she creates is the work of someone who knows exactly which notes to hit.'
— Chris Power, *Guardian*

'With a nimble command of the novel's technical resources and an uncanny grasp of the irrational forces at work in society, [*Paradais* and *Hurricane Season*] navigate a reality riven by violence, race, class, and sex. And they establish Melchor, who was born in 1982, as the latest of Faulkner's Latin American inheritors, and among the most formidable.'
— Juan Gabriel Vásquez, *New Yorker*

'Fernanda Melchor has more than proven herself to be one of the most unmissable voices in translation.'
— Barry Pierce, *Irish Times*

'A masterpiece of concision ... *Paradais* is a labyrinthine monologue on the banal violence of a modern-day teenager.'
— Virginie Despentes, author of *Vernon Subutex*

'Melchor is an incredibly gifted writer.'
— Justin Torres, *New York Times*

'Whereas *Hurricane Season* opens with the corpse, the leaner *Paradais* presses towards calamity. But Melchor's sui generis prose is equally mesmeric here. Disfigured by slang and profanity, her unruly sentences probe the boundary between the graphic and the pornographic. Like the harsh cãna Polo downs, it demands unshrinking imbibement, brooking no pause to reflect on its mechanics or to indulge uneasy doubts about whether the qualities that rivet you are purely literary ones.'
— Lola Seaton, *New Statesman*

'Fernanda Melchor's method is not to produce shocks but to make violence as endemic in her writing ... Rhythm and lexis work in tandem to produce a savage lyricism. The translator Sophie Hughes marvellously matches the author in her pursuit of a new cadence.... an extraordinary feat of control, making [this] exceptional novel into a contemporary masterpiece.'
— Miranda France, *TLS*

'While her writing turns an unsparing eye on the dysfunction and violence of her native Veracruz, Melchor makes clear that it is neither her job nor her intention to explain her homeland. Her novels are less portraits of Mexico than they are literary MRIs, probing unseen corners of the human heart and finding that many of its darker shades are universal.'
— Benjamin P. Russell, *New York Times*

'One of the most talented and innovative novelists around.'
— Michael Delgado, *iNews*

Praise for *Hurricane Season*

'Brutal, relentless, beautiful, fugal, *Hurricane Season* explores the violent mythologies of one Mexican village and reveals how they touch the global circuitry of capitalist greed. This is an inquiry into the sexual terrorism and terror of broken men. This is a work of both mystery and critique. Most recent fiction seems anaemic by comparison.'
— Ben Lerner, author of *The Topeka School*

'This is the Mexico of Cormac McCarthy's *Blood Meridian* or Roberto Bolaño's *2666*, where the extremes of evil create a pummeling, hyper-realistic effect. But the "elemental cry" of Ms Melchor's writing voice, a composite of anger and anguish, is entirely her own.'
— Sam Sacks, *Wall Street Journal*

'Melchor's long, snaking sentences make the book almost literally unputdownable, shifting our grasp of key events by continually creeping up on them from new angles. A formidable debut.'
— Anthony Cummins, *Observer*

'Fernanda Melchor's deep drill into violence, femicide, homophobia and misogyny ... is an uncompromisingly savage piece of work: difficult to escape from, built to shock. Yet it's also elating. I was left buoyed up by Melchor's anger, elated because she had shown me things I needed to be faced with.'
— M John Harrison, *Guardian*

'*Hurricane Season* is a tremendously vital piece of work. Searing and urgent and cut through with pain, this is storytelling as reportage; a loud memorial to the unheard victims of a society in crisis. Fernanda Melchor and Sophie Hughes have achieved something remarkable here.'
— Jon McGregor, author of *Reservoir 13*

Fitzcarraldo Editions

PARADAIS

FERNANDA MELCHOR

Translated by
SOPHIE HUGHES

To Luis Jorge Boone
To Darío Zalapa

'What will happen? Nothing will happen. Nothing could possibly happen. What will I do ... Fall in love knowing that all is lost and there is no hope.'
— José Emilio Pacheco, *Battles in the Desert* (translated by Katherine Silver)

'I hear those sirens scream my name.'
— David Lynch, 'Up in Flames'

It was all fatboy's fault, that's what he would tell them. It was all because of Franco Andrade and his obsession with Señora Marián. Polo just did what he was told, followed orders. Fatboy was completely crazy about her, and Polo had seen first-hand how for weeks the kid had talked about nothing but screwing her, making her his, whatever it took; the same shit over and over like a broken record, his eyes vacant and bloodshot from the alcohol and his fingers sticky with cheesy powder, which the fat pig only ever licked clean once he'd scoffed the whole jumbo bag of crisps. I'll fuck her like this, he'd drawl, having clambered to his feet at the edge of the dock; I'll fuck her like this and then I'll flip her on all fours and I'll bang her like this, and he'd wipe the drool from his mouth with the back of his hand and grin from ear to ear with those toothpaste ad teeth of his, big, white and straight and also clenched in rage as his gelatinous body wobbled in a crude pantomime of coitus and Polo looked away and laughed feebly and made the most of fatboy being distracted to swipe the bottle, light another cigarette and blow the smoke hard up into the air to repel the ferocious mangrove mosquitos. It was all just fatboy's idea of a joke, just banter, drunk talk, or that's what Polo had thought in the beginning, during their first benders down by the river, in the shadiest part of the small wooden platform that ran parallel to the water, just beyond the reach of the poolside lights and where the fig tree's gnarled shadows kept them hidden from the development's night watchman and residents, most crucially Franco's grandparents who, according to Franco, would have a stroke if they caught their 'little boy' consuming alcoholic drinks and smoking cigarettes and God knows what other crap; and worse still, in the company of a member of 'the service' – as that idiot Urquiza called the development's employees – the gardener, no less; an out and out scandal, an abuse of trust that would cost Polo his job, which didn't really bother him anyway because he'd gladly never set foot inside that fucking development again; the problem was that sooner or later he'd have to go home to have it out with his mother, and while that was an awful – not to say downright chilling – prospect, Polo still couldn't help himself. He could never say no to that lard-ass when he waved at him from his window; he didn't want to put an end to their drinking sessions down on the dock no matter how much that prick did his head in, no matter how sick Polo was of his bullshit and his endless obsession with the neighbour, who fatboy had fallen for that afternoon in late May when the Maroños drove into the Paradais residential development to pick up the keys to their new home, Señora Marián herself at the wheel of their white Grand Cherokee.

Polo remembered that day well: he had chuckled to himself on seeing the husband relegated to the passenger seat when the front window rolled down with a buzz and a waft of icy air hit his sweaty face. The woman raised her sunglasses, which otherwise completely obscured her eyes and reflected Polo's face back at him, while she explained who they were and what they were doing there, her lips painted a scandalous red and her bare arms covered in silver bangles that tinkled like wind chimes when Polo finally raised the boom barrier and she thanked him with a wave of her hand. A run-of-the-mill *doña*, pretty standard, he'd never seen the appeal. Identical to all the other women who lived in the development's white villas with those fake terracotta roofs: never without their sunglasses, always fresh and glowing behind the tinted windows of their giant SUVs, their hair straightened and dyed, their nails impeccably manicured, but nothing out of this world when you got up close; Christ, nothing to

14

lose your shit over like fatboy had. Honestly, she was nothing special. You'd probably recognize her from the photos; the husband was famous, had his own TV show, and the four of them were always in the celebrity rags: the bald short-ass of a husband in a suit and long-sleeved shirt, even in the baking heat; the two prissy kids; and her, stealing the limelight with her red lips and those sparkling eyes that seemed to smile at you in secret, somehow both playful and malevolent, her eyebrows raised in coquettish complicity, taller than her husband in her platform shoes, one hand on her hip, her shoulder-length hair loose and her neck draped in eye-catching necklaces. That was the word for her: more than pretty she was eye-catching, striking, made to be looked at somehow, with her gym-sculpted curves and her legs bare all the way up to her thighs, dressed either in raw silk skirts or pale linen shorts that set off the bronze glow of her permanently tanned skin. A passable piece of ass, let's say, each to his own; a decent piece of ass who did a reasonable job of disguising her mileage, the wrinkles and stretchmarks from bearing her two boys – the eldest now all grown up – with creams, designer clothes and that perfectly controlled, metronomic sway of hers, whether she was in heels, sandals or barefoot on her lawn, which made half the residents in Paradais turn to watch her as she passed. Which was exactly what she wanted, right? To be desired, lusted after, to put dirty thoughts into your head. You could tell she loved it, as did her follicly-challenged husband; as far as Polo could see, the guy never took his hands off her, was permanently clutching her waist or stroking her back or feeling up her ass with the smug satisfaction of someone marking his territory and showing off his conquest, while she just smiled away, lapping up the attention, which is exactly why Polo always resisted the urge to look at her, why he always overcame the involuntary twitch he felt in his neck, the almost mechanical pull that demanded he turn his head in the direction of that pert ass as it bounced around the development, mainly because he didn't want anyone – not her, and not her husband or Urquiza either, but especially not that bitch – to catch him looking at her, peering through squinted eyes, drooling open-mouthed like that retard fatboy gawking at her from afar. It was so *obvious* he was crazy about her; he was useless at hiding it. Even Polo had noticed, and at that point, in late May, back when the Maroños moved in to number seven, Polo had yet to hang out with Franco Andrade; there had been no mention of any party for that brat Micky, and the pair of them had never exchanged a word. But it was pretty impossible not to notice fatboy when you came across him roaming the cobbled streets of Paradais, always alone, always dragging his feet, with that formidable belly of his, that rosy face covered in whiteheads and those blond curls that made him look ridiculous, like an overfed cherubin; a monstrous manchild whose soulless eyes only lit up when they hit upon Maroño's wife, who he hadn't stopped stalking since they moved in. You had to be blind or thick as shit not to see the desperate attempts the poor sucker made just to be near her. Any time his neighbour went out into her front garden to play with her sons – usually in Lycra shorts and a sports bra that ended up pasted to her skin from their water fights – that greasy white boy would fly out of his house to pretend he had to clean his grandparents' car, a chore he actually despised, but which these days he did without the old pair having to yell at him or threaten to take away his phone or computer like before. And what a coincidence, too, that every time Señora Marián went down to the pool to sunbathe in her swimsuit, fatty fatso would magically appear three minutes later, squeezed into some trunks which he paired with a t-shirt the size of a tent, his attempt to cover the overspilling tub of lard of his belly, and sunglasses to conceal his fixated gaze on the sun-creamed flesh of Señora Marián lying two sunbeds away, oblivious to fatboy's lubricious sighs and the clumsy prick's fumbling attempts to rearrange his trunks and conceal his little stiffy. But most pathetic of all were his repeated attempts to befriend Señora Marián's two children, reedy Andrés and the spoiled cry-baby Miguel, better known among the other residents as *Andy* and *Micky*, a grotesque display of tastelessness actually encouraged by the Maroños, who the fuck knows why when they didn't have a gringo gene between them, the pricks just couldn't help themselves; and fatboy was even more ridiculous, calling after them in the play area, panting away like a buffalo after the ball that Andy kept dummying, or squirming around Micky, pandering to his every whim, and all to earn the right to be invited to his neighbours' house for afternoon tea and as such to enjoy, however briefly, the company of the woman of his dreams, queen and star of his filthiest sexual fantasies, the rightful owner of the gloopy torrent that gushed from the fawning creep every single night, sometimes well into the early hours, as he pictured her in his mind's eye, her blow-job lips, her plump ass, her sumptuous tits; unable to sleep for the longing, the desire that had overwhelmed him since he first saw her step out of her white SUV, the bubbling sensation that reminded him of the champagne his grandparents drank each New Year's Eve and that fatboy took little sips of whenever they weren't looking; a dizzy feeling, which in her absence turned to anguish and emptiness, a tectonic rift that opened up in his soul every evening when he would be forced to leave his neighbours' house because Señor Maroño had arrived home from work and the boys needed to have their baths and finish their homework and Señora Marián would ask him, in her sweetest, warmest voice, to head home, it was late and his grandma and grandpa must be wondering where he was, and she would give him a playful pat on the back before accompanying him to the front door with a smile, and fatboy would have no choice but to go home with his tail between his legs and Señora Marián's scent – according to him, a mixture of Carolina Herrera, menthol cigarettes and the slightly sour smell of the sweat beads on her cleavage – still wafting around his nostrils, to try, in vain, to fill that growing void with reality TV shows and lewd cartoons that his grandparents disapproved of, and piles of processed biscuits and cakes and huge great bowls of cereal drenched in milk, to then slip away upstairs and lock himself in his air-conditioned room, farting and watching porn on his new laptop that the old pair had bought him for his last birthday and whose storage was already clogged up with smutty films that Franco downloaded from forums and select websites, images of tits, gashes and asses that had actually begun to annoy him, but which he looked at all the same, out of habit, for hours on end. What else could he do to cool the burning passion inside him?

Because ever since Señora Marián arrived on the scene something strange had been going on with fatboy: all his porn suddenly seemed shit, grotesque, a sham; the little hoes who spread their legs, the guys who fucked them, all of them plastic and perfunctory in their moves, a complete and utter let-down, meaningless. The dark-skinned lady with the short hair, for instance, the one he'd lusted after for months – worshipped even, because of her supposed predilection for teenage virgins – now seemed like your average crack whore, too young to play a convincing cougar, but also devoid of the grace and class that positively oozed from Señora Marián, even as she performed the most mundane activities: he only had to see her lean against the kitchen counter as she spoke to a friend on the cordless phone, a cigarette balanced lightly between her slender fingers, the top of her bare foot gliding back and forth over the silky smooth surface of her toned calf. In another league entirely from those fake bitches who, until recently, Franco had lusted after with demented pubescent passion; like that other one, the first on a long list of porn stars that fatboy had obsessed over since he was eleven and his grandparents installed the Internet at home: the mature blond with blue eyes who would shriek and giggle, her pendulous pink tits swinging in the air while a group of thugs took turns to bang her. How many manic wanks had Franco devoted to that old skank, the same one who now, when he returned to those films, the oldest in his computer's hard drive, looked to him like a haggard witch, terrifying and repulsive, her teeth chipped and her mottled skin streaked with greenish veins like a gecko! A world away from Señora Marián's golden complexion as she sunbathed on her front beside the pool, the straps on her bikini top untied to avoid getting tan lines on her divine back, and that succulent rump, gloriously positioned in Franco's eyeline, so real and so close that he would only have to swim to the edge of pool and reach out a hand to feel for himself its peachy smoothness: the most perfect ass, an ass that reduced all the world's asses to nothing, and which, one day, who knew how or when, would be his, his alone to fondle and squeeze and bite and lick and pound without mercy until she yelped with pleasure and fright, repeating his name, *Franco*, his cock driven in as far as it could go, *Franco*, begging for him to give it to her harder, *Harder, Franco, harder, papacito*, until she exploded into multiple orgasms and he gushed warm semen all over her before pushing back inside her, nonstop, all night in his twisted head, and all day too when given the chance, when his grandparents went down to the club on the weekends and fatboy could shut himself in his room without anyone getting on his case, plug in his earphones and settle down to watch his porn, making little mental edits to his old favourites, adding scenes of his own nasty concoction, superimposing Señora Marián's face onto the performers' filthy mugs, his cock like a rod in his hand, his trousers down by his ankles, muttering her name over and over, invoking her, his thighs and his eyelids clamped shut, his teeth clenched, crossing the distance separating them like a ghost that suddenly peeled itself from the fat lump sprawled out on the bed and flew, weightless, through his bedroom window and the walls of the neighbours' house, searching everywhere until he found her sitting in the living room with her husband and two sons: he at one end of the sofa and she at the other, the two squirts in between, propped up by cushions, the youngest's head nestled into one of Señora Marián's delicious tits, faintly visible under her light slip, the kid's drowsy mouth almost grazing her dark nipple showing through the fabric, a button of soft flesh that goes hard when Franco touches it with his invisible hands, timidly at first, then harder when he hears her heave a sigh and shift in her seat, turned on by the tingling sensation that suddenly becomes rougher, wetter, an ectoplasmic mouth that greedily sucks and bites until finally she lets out an involuntary moan. What was going on? she would ask herself. Why was she suddenly dripping wet? Why was her chest pounding from this new pleasure when she was simply sitting in her living room watching a gameshow with her husband and children? And what the hell was that, forcing her thighs apart, penetrating her with delicious violence and making her clench her fists and wriggle in her seat and finally climax with a strangled moan before the stunned faces of her family? Franco's cock would be throbbing and a ribbon of cum would squirt from the tip, wrapping itself around his numb fingers, which were suddenly no longer Señora Marián's tight cunt or puckered asshole, but his own chubby fingers, covered in gunge and cheese powder; impatient fingers that would promptly creep back to his groin and resume their compulsive tugging, Franco this time imagining he was alone with Señora Marián on the Maroños' marital bed, she perched on the edge, Franco standing with his hands in his pockets and his head cocked to one side having just dared confess his secret to her: his longing, his anguish, and the shame he felt admitting it to her, the feeling that he would die if he didn't give in to his desire soon, while Señora Marián nodded away, sweet and obliging, and held out a slender hand to touch Franco's penis through his clothes. He had nothing to worry about, she would tell him, rubbing his bulging erection over the fabric of his shorts. Of course she understood what Franco was going through: a beast like that, so big and so hard, had to be fed, and regularly, she explained to him in that sweet voice she used to soothe her boys when they threw tantrums. He'd done the right thing by telling her; she would help him any time he asked, and with her delicate hands she would undo his belt and take down his underpants and proceed to tug him off, gently but with gusto, wrapping her beautiful, manicured fingers around his entire penis, from the base of the shaft right to the tip, giddy with affection and excitement, while Franco clenched his teeth and his hips juddered in wild spasms that sprayed all over the smiling face of Señora Marián, whose deep-red mouth was half open, continuing on like that for hours on end, one fantasy after the other – he would take her by surprise, naked in the pool, or on the kitchen floor with her hands and feet tied-up, or fresh out of the shower, her pubic hair wet and her nipples hard – until the burning in his urethra would force him to stop all the rubbing and he would finally doze off, the anguish momentarily drained from his body, at least until the following morning when the first thing he always did on opening his eyes was to run to his bedroom window to catch his Lycra-clad neighbour leave her house and climb into her SUV to drop the kids at school, the two brats looking like a pair of drips in their uniforms and visibly disgruntled, before heading to the gym or the beauty salon to do her girly things, which Franco would've loved to have seen first-hand, keeping her company, or just following her in a car, like a spy from the movies.

But there was no way his grandparents were going to lend him their car just like that, even though fatboy had a licence and everything; his father had taught him how to drive when he was really young. The problem was the old farts were still furious at him for having been expelled from school, so furious they even cancelled the trip to Italy his grandma had been planning for months, and in its place they now wanted to visit some horrific military academy in Puebla that promised to bring fatboy to heel in less than six months. They'd also banned him from going to parties and wouldn't pay him his monthly allowance, although fatboy always found a way to squeeze something out of them, hunting around in his grandfather's wallet the second the doddery prick looked away, or lifting items from his grandmother's velvet jewellery boxes, safe in the knowledge that she'd blame their absence on the latest in a long train of housemaids who filed through that house, none of them putting up with the old sour-puss for long. Months would pass before she realised those cheap gold chains and tacky earrings gifted to her by some penniless relative were missing: tat that she never used and that fatboy would pawn on the sly at the nearby shopping mall where they occasionally went for a family breakfast; petty fucking theft, frankly, which fatboy talked up as if he'd held up a bank, possibly to impress Polo, to make him think Franco Andrade was a big tough guy who could do whatever he liked, a gnarly gangster, a rebel with no respect for social norms or decency, when in reality Polo's sole opinion of fatboy was that he was a pain in the ass, a spoiled little rich kid who was only good for one thing: beating his meat all fucking day thinking about his neighbour's ass, and she wasn't even half as hot as the kid made out, although Polo never told him so.

Polo never told fatboy anything during their drinking sessions; he never shared what he really thought of him or his ridiculous fantasies about Señora Marián, at least not in the beginning, during their first meetings down by the dock, when fatboy would get hammered and spend *hours* telling Polo whatever filthy shit went through his head, sparing no details and without a hint of embarrassment: about the porn he watched and how many times a day he masturbated, or the things he'd do to Señora Marián when he finally got his hands on her, by whatever means necessary, while Polo just nodded and chuckled along and shiftily downed three quarters of the bottle of rum that fatboy had paid for, humouring the fat prick but never opening his mouth unless it was to drink from his plastic cup or exhale his cigarette smoke up into the sky to chase away the mosquitos that swarmed in vertiginous clouds above their heads, occasionally nodding to give fatboy the impression that he was listening to him, that he 'got' him, and that he wasn't just there for handouts, right? He wasn't there for the bottle of Bacardi, the six-pack of beers sweating in the heat or the cigarettes, and certainly not to avoid going home sober with his mother and slut of a cousin still up and waiting for him.

That's why he did it, in fact. That's why he always took his sweet time listening to the security guards gossiping instead of rushing straight home to Progreso. That's why he agreed to fatboy hiding the money in the ixoras that grew around the Andrades' front garden and then sending Polo a signal from his bedroom window to go and collect it. Sometimes it was banknotes Polo found; some-times just coins. It didn't make much difference either way because he'd pick up the money, jump on his bike and race down to the convenience store and return with something to get them wasted: a bottle of spirits with some mixers, plus plastic cups when the money stretched to that, cans of beer and filterless cigarettes when they were on special offer, or just a quarter litre of aguardiente and a big carton of orange juice when funds were really low. Polo's poison was white rum and Coke, but once he got going he'd pretty much drink whatever was going, as long as it left his head buzzing and his body numb. When he reached that point, he no longer cared about the bullshit spilling from fatboy's mouth, or the stifling air that seeped from the mangrove like sweat, or the black-flies' and the midges' sly onslaught, or the sinister presence of the mansion rustling their backs, a ram-bling mass of bricks hidden in the undergrowth on the abandoned plot that Polo had to cross to reach the dock whenever he met up with fatboy, the only way to sneak back into the Paradais residential development once he'd clocked off for the day. Convincing the storekeepers to sell him alcohol without either a voter ID or a driving licence was a breeze, since Polo was tall and surly, and looked older than he was; the hard part was getting back in to Paradais without being seen by the cameras or guards, cutting across the neighbouring lot, overgrown with vines and all kinds of plants, until he reached the river, where the sturdy branches of a gnarled fig tree created a bridge for the dock that he could cross without even getting his shoes wet. The problem was that to reach the fig tree Polo had to walk past the Countess's mansion – two storeys of mouldy ruin and the topic of countless stories in town – just as the sun would start to sink behind the strip of palm trees that ran along the opposite bank, stretching shadows all around him and filling the air with strange crackles and fretful shrieks from birds announcing their departure. And he would have to walk right beside the derelict black bay windows of that house, pushing his bike by the handlebars, the plastic bag full of booze swinging and clinking, his eyes boring into the carpet of dry leaves that crunched underfoot so he didn't have to look at the house. He knew he wouldn't see any ghost peeping out of its empty window frames, no spectral hand waving at him to come closer; he knew that mysterious clicking sound was the plaintive call of mourning geckos nestled inside the múcara stone walls of the house, and that the eerie rustling that made the hairs on the back of his neck stand up was just the rattle of the guaje tree's slim pods in the evening river breeze. He was fully aware there was no real menace lurking inside that ruin, no pit of hungry crocodiles hidden among its grimy walls and rapacious ferns, but, man, was it hard to get the stories out of his head, the stories about the Bloody Countess that the old gossips in Progreso had told him when he was little older than a baby, and the truth was that the only thing that ever stopped him from ditching the bike and plastic bag with the booze inside and bolting, terrified, from that place was how much of a fag he'd look if anyone saw, so instead he'd muster the courage to keep going and creep his way through the overgrown parcel until he reached the fig tree on the banks of the river, never once looking back or biting his lips like a coward: he wasn't going to let any little snoops see him and piss themselves laughing at his gutlessness. That's why he only ever started drinking once he was safely on the dock: he'd sooner endure that bitch of a thirst than the fear of being spotted by one of the residents or that prick Urquiza. Once there he would crack open a beer, or on a good day take a good glug directly from whichever bottle of hard stuff he'd been able to afford, and wait for the warm, cottony relief to envelop his entire body, cushioning him from the world's sharp edges, and he'd pull out a cigarette from its fresh packet and light it with his eyes fixed on the Jamapa's lazy course, on the dun waters periodically cut across by the early-riser bats, until eventually his heart would stop racing and Polo would finally pluck up the courage to turn around and take a quick, casual look at the ruin, partially hidden by the ceiba and avocado trees that grew wild there, to make sure that the broken windows were still just empty holes, that no bloody face was peering out from them, and after that he would give a little chuckle of relief, take another slug of his drink and notice, to his delight, that the lights in Progreso, on the other side of the river, were flickering on, and all the terror he'd felt getting across that abandoned parcel, all the tiredness in his aching muscles, even the bad luck that seemed to have followed him ever since his grandfather died, it would all vanish into thin air as he let out a long, deeply felt yawn. Leaning against the fig tree's thick branch, he would close his eyes and breathe in the hyacinths' faint perfume, at which point, never intentionally but unable to stop himself, he would make the same fucking mistake that he always did when he felt happy: the mistake of wishing that moment of solitary peace would never end. Because, of course, at that very moment fatboy would invariably make his appearance on the dock, panting like a pachyderm from the effort of walking down the development's wooden steps, with that witless toothpaste ad grin spread across his face, spouting the same old shit, literally the same bullshit about how he planned to fornicate with Señora Marián, by whatever means necessary, drive it all the way in, no spit, etcetera, sad fucking delusions that hardly even made sense because it didn't take a psychic to see that it was never going to happen, that it was totally ridiculous and impossible to imagine a woman that up herself spreading her legs for a revolting chump like Franco Andrade. Not in his wettest fucking dreams! Polo would think, choking on his cigarette smoke to conceal his laughter while fatboy just carried on running through his little fantasies, at which point Polo really would start caning the bottle, because the more fatboy chinned on, the more Polo could put away, and that was how it'd always been, ever since their first drink together, in the dying hours of brattish Micky's birthday party, that evening in June when Polo had it up to his fucking neck with Paradais and the residents and that idiot Urquiza and he felt like jacking the whole fucking thing in, when fatboy offered him a swig of whisky down on the dock where Polo had escaped to get away from the commotion of the party and to smoke the magnificent cigarette end – almost an entire cigarette, cleanly stubbed out and with no disgusting lipstick marks on the filter – that he'd picked up off the ground, and above all so that Señora Marián couldn't get him to jiggle the piñatas for the entertainment of the stupid kids. He needed to get away from the crowd for a while, smoke his cigarette in peace, take his time with it, but when he bounded down the steps and landed on the dock, he came upon fatboy hogging his favourite hideout, dressed in tight-fitting swimming trunks, his bare feet dangling above the water, and for a moment, for one awkward moment that lasted several seconds, Polo thought that porker was crying because his broad shoulders were shaking and his blue eyes – when he eventually looked up to find Polo looking back at him – were bloodshot and shining wet. And Polo was about to turn right back around and leave the guy to his nancy boy shit when he noticed the bottle on his lap and a wicked smile on his chubby face. Want some? fatboy asked in his jarring falsetto. I'll give you a swig for a smoke, he said, but Polo didn't reply, he just stood staring at the bottle, at the label that he'd seen before, on another bottle just like that one, a bottle he'd nearly tripped on getting into Milton's pickup the last time they'd seen each other, before Milton skipped town again to go work with *them*. Best whisky on the goddamn planet, his cousin – basically his brother – had said when Polo picked up the bottle. Liquid fuckin' gold, *papi*, Milton had said: the only brand his bosses would touch, which they imported by the boxload directly from England; a world away from the beer and Charanda rum that he and Milton used to drink out the back of Doña Pacha's store, although with things as they were, Polo would have happily accepted any drink, literally anything, he might have even managed a few swigs of rotgut, the infamous aguardiente his grandfather used to make from pure alcohol and the fly-infested fruits from the nanche tree in the yard outside their house, because it had been nearly a month since Polo had touched a drop of alcohol, since he'd made the stupid fucking mistake of promising his mother he wouldn't get drunk again, or rather, since his mother had made him promise that he wouldn't drink again. And for twenty-six days he'd valiantly resisted, the main reason being that his mother pocketed his entire salary, but also because there was still no sign of Milton in town, and in any case his new life as a hard-working, responsible employee prevented him from hanging out at the back of Pacha's, where he would've been able to sponge a few *caguamas* off someone even if he was broke; but the truth was that, for all his promises, not a single day went by when Polo didn't think about getting on it, and that evening in early June, in the middle of that retard Micky Maroño's party, he'd reached the end of his patience and all he could think about was sticking two fingers up to them all, quitting his miserable, piss-pay job and punching that idiot Urquiza on his way out, a quick one-two to his smug fucking egghead: who'll wash your car now, you fucking faggot; let's see which other dickhead agrees to stay late cleaning this shitheap for free. Fucking criminal, that's what it was, being made to spend whole hours waiting for the residents and the shitty hangers-on to leave so that he could start clearing up their filthy shit: their empty beer cans, their greasy napkins, their paper plates full of leftovers, and all the cigarette butts they'd crushed underfoot or even left floating in the illuminated cobalt blue pool. What would it cost people to put their rubbish in one of the bins that were dotted literally all around the pool area? Nothing, the truth was it wouldn't cost them anything, but why should they bother when Polo was around, their loyal *muchacho*, waiting in the shadows with a giant black bag in his hand, bored out of his brains, salivating over the peppery smell of grilled meat and the vision of metal buckets brimming with ice cubes and beers, waiting for them to leave so he could finally start cleaning up their mess. Urquiza had been quite clear since Polo's very first day in that dead-end job: it was the gardener's responsibility to ensure that the swimming pool was clear of leaves, insects and any other litter at all times, that the poolside was swept and tidied, that the furniture was put back in its place first thing in the morning so that the early birds among the residents – Franco's ancient, fussy grandparents included, of course – could soak their pasty skin in the dew-freshened water, even if that meant Polo had to stay on until eleven or twelve at night on weekends, or whenever the beaming partygoers finally dragged their asses home, and Polo had had enough. And although it was true that on the whole he looked for any excuse to put off going home, Polo couldn't stand the utter brazenness with which Urquiza broke the contract Polo had signed just weeks earlier in which it clearly stated that the services he would render for the Gulf Real Estate Company Ltd would correspond to the position of gardener, with working hours between seven a.m. and six p.m. with one hour for lunch at midday, and that any activity undertaken outside of those hours would be duly remunerated, a clause which that asshole Urquiza happily wiped his ass with whenever it meant he could save the Company a peso or two, or even pocket them himself if Polo was to believe the security guards, on whom, apparently, Urquiza regularly pulled the same stunt; you'd better keep your head down if you want to keep the job, Cenobio would say, so Polo just sucked it up, even though it meant slogging his guts out all day long, watering and mowing the lawn, pruning the trees and bushes in the communal gardens, strimming the hedges and flowerbeds, sweeping the dead leaves from the four cobbled streets of that gated community, thrashing away the sand that built up along the kerbs on windy days, scraping and repainting the salt-corroded lights, killing any gophers that dared dig up the lawns, taking care of the dog turds that the loafing residents were incapable of picking up themselves with their immaculate hands when they took their dogs out, keeping the pool and surrounding areas impeccable, and, on top of all that – and this really made Polo's blood boil – every day without fail washing Urquiza's car, all because he could make him, and because it gave the lazy prick a boner to see his red Golf sparkling like it was 'hot off the forecourt'. But don't take too long, yeah? Just give her a quick rinse when you get a chance, no rush, okay, no pressure, and then the grinning prick would throw Polo the keys so he could vacuum the inside as well. The urge Polo felt to smash those keys into his stupid face and tell him: wash it yourself, asshole, before whipping out the machete at his waist and bringing it down on that big bald head! Polo wasn't a violent person, he wasn't prone to angry outbursts, you could ask anyone: they'd all say Polo was an easy-going sort, that he had no beef with anyone and never got involved in other people's shit; the thing was Urquiza really took the piss, he thought he had a monopoly on Polo's time because he saw him as a little boy, an inexperienced hick, and the prick acted like he was doing Polo a favour giving him that gig, but Polo wasn't falling for it, he knew it was a gross injustice; it wasn't just in his head, he wasn't just making up excuses to be lazy or stirring up trouble for the hell of it, as his mother insisted he was every time she heard him whine about the job, sometimes without Polo having said anything at all but because she found him sighing miserably in the kitchen, sitting at the table, watching two Alka-Seltzers dissolving in a glass of water, Polo's breakfast of champions that gave him the strength to face another day of back-breaking work under the sun's rays, in this, his new life as an employee of the Gulf Real State Company S. A. de C. V., where his mother had worked since she was sixteen, first as a housemaid in the chief engineer's house, then as a cleaner in the company's office development, and finally, after taking endless evening courses in the centre of Boca, as an assistant accountant. That's what they pay you for, his mother would lecture him each morning, to do what they say and keep your trap shut; who cares what shit they get you to do, that's what they hired you for: to do as they say not to drag your lazy ass around grumbling. You've barely got your foot in the door and already you want them to make you the boss, when you don't have a clue. Not such a tough guy now, eh, Polo? Oh, you're the big man when you're out on the lash, but when it comes to putting in the hours you never lift a finger. You should be ashamed of yourself. The world won't just land at your feet, sunshine, you have to graft, really graft, and not turn your nose up at the first job you don't like. Or I suppose you'll tell me it's my fault they kicked you out of school? Come on, tell me, was I the one who made you skive off and flunk every single subject because you were out getting legless? You had your chance to learn something, Polo, a better chance than me or your poor grandfather, rest his soul, and you fucked it up, sunshine, you fucked it up because you're a born shirker, so now it's your turn to break your back, and his mother would go on and on, the same shit, every single morning, whether he'd complained about work or not, she only had to get the faintest whiff of the pathetic resignation Polo gave off just thinking about getting up from the breakfast table, onto his bike and cycling over to Paradais.

That's why he'd been about to jack it all in that Saturday, not just because he'd been made to stay until the end of that brat Micky's party to clean up the filthy dregs, but because of something that had happened to him earlier that day, hours before the piñatas were brought out, when Polo was by the pool clearing leaves from the water's surface with a net, lost in a world of his own as a whole squad of catering company staff darted back and forth across the garden, setting up tables and chairs and gazebos and even a long colourful tarp, which, when plugged in to a pump, transformed into an imposing bouncy castle, a formidable thing with towers and battlements and flags and chutes and even a drawbridge; a colossal yet volatile, ethereal structure that took off each time the breeze blew in from the river, as if it wanted to escape, and Polo was so entertained watching the staff struggle to pin down the castle with straps and pegs that he didn't notice Señora Marián appear until he smelled her perfume in the air, at which point he turned around to find her standing right in front of him, her body just inches from his, her lips blood-red like a vampire's and her face blushing, missing the trademark sunglasses that instead were hanging from a thin gold chain between her tits. She was wearing jeans and had something in her hands, a small manilla envelope that she held out to Polo without a word, stretching her shameless smile even wider when she saw that the boy couldn't take it because he was holding the long pool skimmer in both hands, and eventually slipped into the front pocket of his overalls herself with a giggle and a 'for your trouble' muttered with false modesty before turning around and sashaying off to oversee the work of her newly acquired maid, a mousy, emaciated-looking girl who in that very moment was clumsily throwing herself into the task of decorating the party chairs with covers and bows. Polo had the feeling he knew her, that he'd seen her before, at school maybe, but he didn't dare look for long, he didn't want his employer to think he was looking at her, so he went back to the business of cleaning the pool, feigning composure and resisting the urge to put his hands in his overall pocket and touch the envelope to gauge what was inside, at least until lunchtime came around, at which point he could lock himself inside the security hut's tiny toilet, take out the envelope with his name written on one side in glittery purple felt-tip pen, and gaze at the two two-hundred peso banknotes contained within it, both crisp and pressed as if fresh from the cash machine: the overtime, plus tip, which the idiot Urquiza always cheated him out of and which Polo moaned about every time he was made to stay late to clean the mess left over from the parties; a nice cash injection, totally unexpected, and he wouldn't have to tell his mother about it either. He could spend every peso on whatever the hell he liked: cigarettes, obviously, a couple of bottles of Bacardi, and, if it stretched to that, some phone credit so he could text Milton to tell him to get in touch. But even as he made plans in his head, excited by the prospect of spending his sudden windfall, he felt an aching in his chest, and moments later he was doubled over the toilet regurgitating bile in violent, spluttering spasms, and all for having remembered the look on that bitch's face as she slipped the envelope into his overall pocket, and the smile that Polo, like some kind of chump, had been obliged to return, against his will, unable to stop the muscles on his face from contracting even though he despised that slut's airs and graces and the barefacedness with which she'd touched him, because, frankly, it was a hundred times easier to resist the urge to check out her ass when she was jogging around the development in hotpants than to overcome the impulse to return one of Señora Marián's smiles, she was that magnetic, that enticing; and they'd instantly know what he was talking about if they'd met her in person and experienced first-hand her powers of seduction. Why the hell hadn't he handed the envelope straight back and told her, with every ounce of disdain he could muster: *I don't need your handouts, thanks very much*? Why hadn't he thrown it back in her face and let her know what he thought of her: that she was nothing but a whore, a gold digger who thought that going around handing out her husband's spare change somehow made her more respectable? And why the hell hadn't she just handed him the money like a normal person? Was she afraid Polo would make her dirty, that he'd infect her with his poor, hick ways? Did the bitch really think she could buy him, that she'd bought the right to demand whatever she wanted of him, to humiliate him like Urquiza, to make him wash her white SUV or her husband's sportscar? Who the fuck did she think she was? The fucking queen bee judging by her outfit that afternoon, when the party began right on time and she appeared wearing a red dress with blue and green polka dots on it and diamond earrings that glinted whenever she flicked her brown hair from her neck. All afternoon Polo did his best to ignore her, but it was as if an invisible force kept putting her in his path; wherever he turned, there she was, lavishing kisses and hugs on the hordes of little boys and girls running around in swimsuits, and on the women dressed head to toe in tropical prints, as svelte and heavily made up as the hostess herself, their hair straight and inert, as neat and lifeless as wigs, and the husbands just as ridiculous in their pink polos and pastel shirts, ankle grazers and brown loafers, with golf tans and perfectly groomed beards and eyebrows, a clique of pompous voices and clinking ice cubes gathered around that smug short-ass Maroño who spent the entire party taking photos and talking politics and business in the puffed-up lingo of professional cocksuckers to a fawning audience who knocked back glass after glass of imported whisky, not even pausing to cop a look at the hostess's sweet behind, all while their offspring screeched and launched themselves at the juddering bouncy castle walls like raving lunatics, and did running cannonballs into the pool, shrieking with suicidal glee yet barely audible over the music blaring from the mounted poolside speakers. And there came a point, at around six in the evening, when Polo frankly couldn't take it any more: the noise, the people, his guts marinading in the juices of his own rage, and above all the hysterical bawling coming from the birthday boy himself, who was face down on the lawn, kicking and wailing at the top of his lungs because it was time for the piñatas but he didn't want anybody to touch them because they were his, and among all that confusion, and before Señora Marián could rope Polo into the demeaning task of jiggling the piñatas like an idiot, Polo took his chance to make a swift exit and disappear behind the barrier that Urquiza had ordered him to position that morning in front of the stairs that led down to the dock, just in case some inquisitive brat tried to go down to the river and fell into the Jamapa's waters, which the residents all believed to be dangerous, infested with bacteria and parasites, and full of perilous pools where their precious offspring could drown; a load of rubbish that Polo took advantage of every so often to sneak down there and enjoy a few moments to himself sitting on that ornamental dock – more an architectural whim than an actual mooring – to watch the river's grey-green waters flow by, and maybe to have a smoke in blessed peace, just as he did on the evening of Micky's birthday when he bounded down the wooden steps in three strides, cigarette end already lit between his lips, and ran into the fat kid with the blond curls sitting on the dock in nothing but his swimming trunks, jelly belly on full display, legs dangling above the water and his head bowed, and for a second, in the half-light of the setting sun, surrounded by that perennial green, Polo thought fatboy was crying, probably over the humiliation he'd been subjected to at the party and which Polo had seen for himself with a degree of sick pleasure because, despite not knowing him personally, the truth was he thought Franco Andrade was a total prick, and he'd been genuinely entertained watching as that little poof Andy and his flotilla of pugnacious teenyboppers laid into fatboy throughout the party, viciously attacking him with almonds, hitting him on the head – mostly on his face – with the rock hard green fruits that those super-brats pulled from the lower branches of the almond trees dotted around the gardens; a cunning assault that lasted several hours and that not one of the adults present tried to stop, maybe because they were too busy polishing off the Maroños' whisky and white wine and chatting shit, or maybe because deep down they too found fatboy ridicu-lous, unbearable, and they too hoped he'd leave, taking his love handles and his weeping pimples and his sad manboobs that wobbled obscenely each time he moved his hips with him, and maybe that's why the guests just sighed with relief when Franco Andrade finally vanished from the party, but not before swiping a bottle of that wanker Maroño's whisky, or at least that's what he told Polo; who the fuck knew if it was true, with fatboy you could never be sure, the guy was a compulsive liar, he got his kicks out of making up the most unbelievable stories

– even if the part about the whisky being Maroño's was true – and with a knowing smile, flashing a perfect set of teeth, he offered Polo a swig in exchange for a smoke, which Polo didn't have, although that wasn't going to stop him getting his hands on that magic potion, which, even from six feet away, he could smell in the air: wood shavings soaked in saltwater, a smell as intense as Polo's craving to wrap his lips around that bottle, and so instead of turning and walking away he moved in closer to the pimply whale calf and offered him his lit cigarette end. It's my last one, he said, his eyes locked on the bottle on the kid's lap. Fatboy greedily smoked the butt and then flicked it into the river, even though there was a whole drag's worth of tobacco left on the filter. Fucking prick, Polo thought as he waited for that lard-ass to raise the bottle to his lips and take a long swig. It's imported, he told Polo, letting out a long moan of pleasure and wiping his lips with the back of his hand and then, finally, passing the bottle to Polo, who drank from it even though he didn't trust fatboy for shit, and even though he'd promised his mother that he wouldn't continue down that path, the path of vice that had been his grandfather's undoing, and Polo drank until he felt that firewater surge through his limbs and fill his body with warm calm, and they passed the bottle back and forth until they'd drained the whole thing, and that was the first time fatboy spoke to Polo about Señora Marián, mentally playing out his little fantasies about one day making her his; and if you asked fatboy he'd tell you he was well on his way to doing just that and that you could tell how much she liked him, how highly she thought of him, from the warmth and admiration in her smiles whenever she greeted him or said goodbye, from the way she was always looking for an excuse to touch him, to kiss his cheek, clear signs that

Señora Marián was into him, right? Signs that she wasn't entirely indifferent, and one of those days something would have to happen between them, wouldn't it? More than anything, Polo found fatboy's delusions fucking hilarious; Christ, he never thought the guy was serious! Had Franco not seen himself in the mirror? Did he really think a woman like Señora Maroño would cheat on her millionaire husband with a tubby spotty greaseball like him? The little fag couldn't even look his neighbour in the eyes, Polo had noticed at the party. He would stare at her from afar, sometimes like a puppy, sometimes like a sick rapist. Was that how he planned to win her over? Even if the old bitch opened the door to him butt naked, as he fantasized, even if she begged him to stick his little pecker in her, even then that stupid prick wouldn't know where to start, not only because it was obvious he'd never been near a wet cunt in his life, but because he clearly didn't have the balls to approach any member of the opposite sex and do what it took to tame her, control her, spread her legs; he didn't have the balls to actually make a move and stop spending his life drooling and pining like a dummy, like the jarring little pussy that he was. That's why Polo played along, that's why he nodded away to everything that fatty said, as insane, as preposterous as it was; how the fuck was he supposed to know what the crazy prick would be capable of doing in order to bone that bitch. Who could have known he really meant what he said?

That's how it all began, he'd tell them. A few days later, when they got plastered again with the money fatboy lifted from his grandparents and passed on to Polo so he could buy booze, cigarettes and those revolting cheesy snacks covered in orange powder, Franco's delicacy. It quickly became a routine: the impatient wait after lunch, the search for the cash in the flowerbeds, the local store packed with labourers having a quick cold drink before heading back to Boca or to their own communities; the nerve-wracking walk through the abandoned plot and its crumbling mansion, meeting each other at sundown on the dock, the boozing and smoking, Franco Andrade wanging on, Polo sniggering to himself, the palliative stupor from the drink, of which there was never as much as Polo would've wanted, scarcely enough to dull the mind, to take the edge off. That's why he drank so fast, almost racing against Franco until the booze had all gone, the cigarettes too, and with them their only means of keeping the hungry mosquitos at bay, until the lights in Progreso on the other side of the river would start to go out, at which point Polo would be sufficiently wasted to head back into the almost pitch darkness of the undergrowth and past the rustling pile, pushing his bike by the handlebars and singing under his breath, *voy a llenarte toda, toda*, any old tune he might've heard on Cenobio's radio, *lentamente y poco a poco*, no matter how cheesy or dumb, *con mis besos*, anything to distract him from the Bloody Countess who built that solitary palace in the estuary's mangrove swamps and whose gruesome silhouette – according to the gossips in Progreso, his mother included of course – would still frighten the wits out of the reckless fools who dared hang around those parts, until finally Polo would emerge onto the deserted track, mount his bike, and coast down the hill until he reached the highway shoulder, sweating copiously from the stifling heat and the effort to keep the handlebars steady so he didn't go crashing head-first into one of the few cars still driving around at that time of night. No matter how much or how quickly he drank down on the dock, it was never enough to knock him out, to send the whole world packing, to switch off completely, be free, and all too quickly the precious trance he'd worked so hard to achieve would dissolve into a throbbing headache that grew more intense each time Polo remembered that in a matter of hours he'd be back cycling along the very same road, ready to begin a new day in poxy Paradais. That's why whenever he crossed the bridge over the river he would stop for a few minutes to watch the brackish waters snake their way between the lawns, the luxury villas on one side, and on the other the tiny islands populated by willows and shaggy palm trees, barely visible against the salmon-pink canvas of the port, all lit up in the night sky, there in the distance, and he would get to thinking about the boat that he and his grandfather should've built together when there was still time, a humble skiff, nothing special, with a pair of powerful oars, or maybe just a simple bargepole to haul their way up the sludgy riverbed until they reached the middle of the estuary teeming with bobo mullet on their way down from the mountains and sea bass heading inland to spawn near the river's mouth. Or that's what his grandfather would always say, before he went and croaked. If he had that boat, Polo thought, he wouldn't have to do those exhausting round trips on his bike back and forth from Paradais to Progreso; or better still, if his grandfather had kept his promise of teaching him how to build a boat, if he'd taken seriously all their dreaming as they fished together on the bridge, Polo would never even have to go back to that fucking place or put up with the shit-packer

Urquiza and his constant put downs: he could earn his living fishing in his boat, or taking tourists out on the lagoon, or just head upriver with no destination, no plans or responsibilities, row his way to one of the towns along the river and its tributaries any time he needed something, and leave again just as freely, with no one to stop him; he wouldn't have to make ridiculous pledges of abstinence or put up with humiliating and totally unreasonable take-downs, he wouldn't have to sleep on the living room floor or be forced to wake at the crack of dawn to his mother's shitty alarm clock jingle, or spend the whole day watering the same fucking lawn, which he'd be back mowing days later; or pedal uphill sandwiched between the luxury urban developments' sky-high walls, all crowned with barbed wire and razor wire, swerving this way and that on the gravelly roadside, blinded by the lights of the cars that seemed to rush headlong in his direction. Maybe the one good thing about returning so late to that house – besides sparing himself his mother's earfuls and Zorayda's slutty glances – was that the highway was all but deserted at that hour so he could cycle along it without having to wait for the evening traffic to calm down, and by the same token use the momentum he picked up to veer into the side road that opened up in the undergrowth, the shortcut that would lead him straight to his house, avoiding Progreso entirely, a dirt track which, at that time of night, was more like a living, breathing pit of darkness, a tunnel that echoed with deathly screeches and the croaks of cicadas and enormous toads hiding in the grass, a track that Polo would turn into without a second thought, without braking at all, befuddled by his thirst and pounding head, squinting from the sweat and insects in his face, pedalling furiously and with drunken abandon and placing all his

trust in his muscle memory, which seemed to remember
the places where the track grew narrow or gnarled with
tree roots after all those years spent cycling back and
forth twice a day through that tunnel of vines and ferns
and boggy leaf mould that stank of fresh grave: first as a
young boy, to attend the school on the other side of the
river, and then, when he was a bit older, to take the bus to
Boca. And now he was back riding the same route day in
day out to get him to and from Paradais, and had been
ever since his mother dragged him to the offices of the
Gulf Real Estate Company to print his full name on the
contract that galling idiot Urquiza put in front of him; a
contract stating that from that day on, Leopoldo García
Chaparro would be employed as the gardener of the urban development Paradise. *Paradais*, Urquiza corrected
Polo the second time he tried to say that gringo shit. It's
pronounced *Pa-ra-dais*, not *Pa-ra-dee-sey*. Listen, repeat
after me: *Paradais*. And the newest employee had wanted
to reply: *Paradais* my ass, you loose fucking faggot, but he
didn't dare say anything with his mother right there beside him, pressuring him to get on and sign it, berating
him with her beady yellow eyes, the watchful eyes of a
hungry grackle. Just sign it, she told her son on noticing
him leaf through the contract. Sign first, then read it, stop
wasting this gentleman's time. And Polo had no choice
but to sign that horse shit, despite the strongest suspicion
that he'd just sold his soul to the devil, a feeling that grew
when he saw how happy his mother was to witness his
transformation into the minion of that bunch of self-
important cunts, because it was about time Polo pulled
his finger out, stopped scratching his balls, he'd never
done a decent day's work in his life, hadn't taken home a
single peso since the almighty clusterfuck – there was no
other word for what he'd gone and done – he'd made of

44

school, flunking all six subjects in the first semester, and all for absences, for throwing her efforts down the drain, the countless sacrifices his mother had made over the years to provide that lazy shit with the opportunities she never had. So now it was his turn to pull his sleeves up, now he could work his ass off for the family and stop being such an irresponsible bum. They didn't have a pot to piss in, and what with his cousin Zorayda's little slip-up, in a few months they'd be more squeezed than ever, assuming the whole town didn't go to shit before then. It was just as well that Señor Hernández the engineer had given Polo his 'big break', the chance to work in one of his residential developments, because Progreso was turning into a den of crooks and Polo ran a very real risk of turning out like his cousin Milton, the shameless little crook who'd led him astray. Where exactly was the pleasure in drinking himself silly? Why didn't he take a leaf out of his grandfather's book? His poor grandfather who'd worked like a dog his whole life to build a future for himself, to provide for them, with no help from anyone, just blood, sweat and tears, toiling from dusk till dawn, never taking a break or making up pathetic excuses, never moaning or pretending to be sick so he didn't have to get up, you waste of space, who do you think you are, Polo? Who the hell do you think you are?

That was the kind of grief Polo woke up to each day, before the sun had even appeared at the window, just as the neighbour's cockerel was clearing its throat to compete with his mother's phone alarm. Polo would grumble and toss and turn on the floor, on the sweat-soaked petate, his mouth dry, his eyes glued together with sleep and his temples throbbing with the headache that now never went away, no matter how many Alka-Seltzers he drank. He would aim to get up and out as early as he could – Lord knows he tried to avoid his mother's sermons – but she always got there first, when he was still on the floor battling his exhaustion, and she would launch straight in: wasn't he ashamed, crawling home in the middle of the night and creeping in to his own house like a thief, and all for a piss-up! Don't lie to me, you little creep, don't you dare lie to your mother! I can smell the stench of booze on you from here, you useless drunk! It's only Wednesday and you're already out getting leathered, just look at the state of your face. Seriously, who do you think you are, Leopoldo? Who the hell do you think you are, you little shit?

There wasn't a day Polo didn't ask himself the same thing, every morning, with a bread roll and a mug of luke-warm coffee in his belly, which, on a good day, he would manage to reach the bridge without chucking up, his overalls laundered but still grubby thanks to Zorayda's inept hands, his face dripping with sweat and the salty wind spray that he pedalled against on his way to Paradais. Who was he, really? A little shit, his mother would say. But *her* little shit, at the end of the day, the 'little miracle' of the girl who got shafted yet still worked her way up in the world. He had her thick lips, the same amber eyes and wiry hair that went coppery in the sun's rays, and now he too was at the service of the same family of sharks. The *muchacho*, as the residents called him, that's who he was: the lawn waterer, the tree pruner, the turd scooper, the car washer, the chump who appeared the second those assholes whistled for him: the dogsbody. How had he sunk so low? he asked himself, without an answer. And how the fuck was he going to get out of there? Again, he didn't know. He had nothing, not a single thing to call his own. Even his salary went straight into his mother's pocket, every last peso, exactly as she'd dictated: Polo owed her, to make up for his colossal fuck-up, the opportunity he'd gone and

pissed down the drain. Now it was his turn to work like
a bitch, to follow Urquiza's ridiculous orders; his turn to
sleep on the floor like a filthy animal while the money he
earned went towards paying off his mother's countless
debts and feeding the baby growing inside Zorayda's horrendous belly, while that slob spent her days lounging on
the rocking chair, watching cartoons – with the fan on, of
course – instead of taking care of the house and cooking
their meals, as they'd agreed. From the start he'd tried to
reason with his mother, make her see how unfair it all was:
first, it wasn't his fault his cousin couldn't keep her legs
shut. Why did he have to give her his bed and sleep on the
floor, on the hard concrete floor with only a thin petate
under his aching body and a rolled up old t-shirt for a
pillow? Why didn't they send Zorayda packing instead?
She was a total pain in the ass, a freeloader, a conniving
bitch who felt no shame waddling around town with a gut
like a pregnant cow as if she'd been blessed with that 'little
miracle' who could belong to just about any guy in town,
genuinely any of them; if only Polo's mother would listen
to the shit people said about her, how the little prick tease
would fool around with the bus drivers, the delivery guys
who stopped by Doña Pacha's store on Tuesdays, the loan
sharks who passed through town on their way to Pado del
Toro, and even with the boys who delivered tortillas on
their mopeds, there wasn't a single one of them she hadn't
rolled about with on the mucky floors of truck cabins,
or on the back seats of cars, or standing bent over like a
bitch in heat behind the storage rooms and animal sheds,
or wherever the urge happened to take her. Why didn't
his mother leave her to sort out her own shit? The little
skank had asked for it. Why didn't she send Zorayda back
to the aunts in Mina, let them clean up her mess? But his
mother wouldn't hear it; her face clouded over whenever

Polo so much as hinted at throwing his cousin out on the street, and she absolutely flew off the handle if he ever dared suggest that slut didn't even want to be a mother, that she probably would have got rid of it if Polo's mother hadn't laid everything out on a silver platter for her like she was royalty, while Polo worked his ass off and slept on the baking, rock-hard floor with just a flimsy old mat under his tired bones.

That's why he got wasted every chance he got, even when it meant doing so in the company of that disgusting lump Franco, and even if he spent the best part of the next day with a pounding head and acid reflux. He had no choice but to get wrecked, because of those two at home, because drinking with fatboy meant he didn't have to go back to Progreso until much later at night, when there'd be no one on the streets apart from the little punks acting as spies for *them* and the odd nocturnal hound; when his mother and Zorayda would be fast asleep and Polo wouldn't have to see them or listen to them or be anywhere near them. He would slip in via the kitchen door, undress in silence and lie down on the scratchy fabric of his petate in the middle of the pitch black living room, always roasting hot from the sun that beat down on their corrugated roof all day, and he would close his eyes and cover his face with one arm and think about the fetid black river flowing beneath the bridge, its unstoppable, captivating course, and the subtle, unassuming perfume of the floating islands of water hyacinths carried on the cool breeze, and suddenly the pitching motion of his drunken state, the rolling floor, became the gentle rise and fall of the river singing beneath his body, the ever-shifting, ever-forgetting current of dark water flowing right out to sea; there he would be, in the boat that he and his grandfather would have built if the old man hadn't gone and died first; a modest craft, but big enough for Polo to be able to lie down and look up at the snippets of sky gliding by through the treetops and woodbine, the din of countless black crickets and the tuneful cries of creepy crawlies fornicating and devouring one another drowned out by the river's overwhelming voice, its cold, indefatigable song, louder at night than at any other time, or that's what Polo's grandfather would tell him back when they used to go fishing at night under the bridge, their rubber boots ankle-deep in the thick mud littered with broken glass, sharp bones and rusty cans, their eyes fixed on the sloping fishing line cast into the misty mirror that was the backwater at that hour; grey and silver in the middle, intense green along the banks where the merciless vegetation overran everything, choking itself in an orgy of climbing tentacles and teeming webs of lianas and thorns and flowers that mummified the young trees then scattered the snags with devil's trumpets and blue bellworts, especially come June, when the rainy season would announce itself with isolated, almighty downpours that only seemed to further charge the stifling evening air and accelerate the growth of the pestilent jungle of plants that sprang up on all sides: shrubs and lianas and woody-stemmed ivy that appeared out of nowhere, green and lush, on the roadsides, or right in the middle of the splendid gardens of Paradais, fruit of the clandestine spores that snuck their way between the sleek blades of perfect lawn, and which, overnight, would unfurl their somehow both exquisite and ordinary leaves for Polo to hack at with his machete, because neither the asthmatic lawnmower nor the electric strimmer could compete against those bastard weeds, which invaded the flowerbeds and central reservations, decimating the begonias and China roses.

Polo liked thrashing through the undergrowth with his

machete, and the feeling of carrying it at his waist as he walked along the development's cobbled streets; he loved slashing the gigantic weeds looming over him with their horned thorns and their furry, spiky leaves; monstrous plants that made him think of extra-terrestrial invaders disguised as harmless shrubs but capable of smothering the entire development, the riverbank, the whole coast even, under a blanket of suffocating green. Sometimes, when Urquiza sent him to clear the development's furthermost limits, and when Polo was absolutely sure noone could see or hear him to laugh at his games, he would launch a bloody attack against the undergrowth, jumping and shrieking and even doing flying kicks when he felt the plants were trying to ambush him, until there was nothing left around him but a carpet of slashed leaf litter and hacked canes bleeding like victims on a battlefield. Staring at the mutilated weeds, puffing and panting from his efforts and with sweat trickling down his brow, Polo would imagine he could see something moving among the hewn foliage: the bejucos stretching out their tender stems, momentarily overcome but undeterred and undefeated in their ultimate aim to keep growing and propagating, conspiring in a rustling tongue, waiting for the moment they would take their revenge. But those ideas of his never lasted long, and Polo knew the gentle stirring of leaves was just the breeze blowing up from the river, or even his own exhausted state combined with the harsh sun beating down on the back of his neck, and pretty soon he would find shelter in a shady spot and take off his cap to fan his puce face, and having finally caught his breath, he would stand up and recommence his savage extermination until either he'd neutralized the plants' advance or a rainstorm would force him to take refuge in the security hut, attended during the day by the oldest guard in the development, a guy called Cenobio with a droopy grey moustache and the air of a docile dog about him, and he and Polo would take it in turns to dash out into the torrential rain and raise the boom barrier for any visitors entering or exiting the development. Unlike Rosalío – the other, younger, mouthier guard – Cenobio wasn't much of a talker, he liked to keep the radio on and tuned into a station playing love songs, and sometimes, when the rain really pelted down, drumming riotously on the security hut's plastic roof, he would open the door, pull out a packet of filterless cigarettes, offer one to Polo and turn up the volume on the radio, and the pair of them would stand next to the open door and watch the spectacle of the deluge. It was almost pleasant, that sudden freshness tempering the midday heat, the distant thunderclaps as the lightning hit the nearby ocean waves, and above all not having anything to do, no watering the grass, or mowing the lawn, or repainting posts, or trapping gophers and moles, or washing that idiot Urquiza's car, or collecting dog shits, because the rain took care of those, liquifying the steaming turds until they dissolved into the grass. Some days, when the downpour didn't stop, by six o'clock Polo would already find himself cycling down the hill to the highway; in part because Urquiza couldn't think of anything else to make him do, but also because fatboy hadn't showed his face since the second week of June, he no longer stood at his bedroom window pointing and signalling at him, and Polo was sure the fat fuck hadn't gone away like so many of the other residents because every now and then, while pruning the ixoras in the Andrade's front garden, Polo would catch Franco's squeaky voice as he argued with his grandparents inside the house. He must've been sick, or maybe just depressed, inconsolable because the Maroños had fucked off on their holidays to the Caribbean and hadn't invited him, as the deluded prick had hoped they would, which meant he'd missed out on a golden opportunity to see Señora Marián trying out brand new bikinis and sarongs, more tanned and horny than ever, and Polo was left with no choice but to fill the evening hours by taking long walks through the sludgy streets in town looking for a familiar face, someone to shout him a smoke, a caguama maybe; someone to chat mindlessly with about the heat and the rainstorms, anything to avoid going home so early, but most of the time Polo just wandered aimlessly, eventually ending up sitting on a faded tree trunk on the sandy river-bank by Milton's house, throwing stones into the water and wondering what the fuck he was going to do. It felt like he had no friends left in Progreso, no acquaintances even, as if everyone his and Milton's age had left town and moved to Boca for good or were in hiding from *them*, and the only ones left in Progreso were kids, little punks younger than Polo, and sloppy bitches with nothing to do, neither of which were much use to Polo: the young kids because they all worked for *them* and thought they were big fucking deals with their handheld radios and their little bags of cocaine cut with laxatives, driving around on their farty little scooters, referring to themselves as 'falcons' when they were more like little squeakers; and the sloppy bitches because it seemed the only thing they cared about was popping out more kids and sitting outside their houses gossiping the whole day long, watching the action out on the street and blowing cheeky kisses at the first cock that happened to swing by. Polo really missed the good old days when, coming out of school – or sometimes not having gone in the first place – he would head over to Milton's or to Doña Pacha's store and his cousin, practically his brother, would share his smokes and beers with him, because Milton was older and he had a job and money to burn, not to mention stories to tell: about his escapades with his brother-in-law who owned the scrapyard on the outskirts of Progreso and was always going down to the southern border in stolen vehicles they'd bought for cheap in the capital and then fixed up to sell in Chiapas or to the Guatemalan mafia. That's why, quite often, sick of wandering around town like a loser, Polo would cycle to Milton's house and jump the enclosing wall, making sure the squeakers didn't see him, half hoping to find some sign that he was back in town and the other half just wanting to see if Milton had left anything lying around that Polo could take and sell for cash to buy some booze, a quarter litre of caña even, but it was more than obvious, from the thick layer of grime and saltpetre on the windows, from the deathly hush inside that place and the freedom with which the spiders span their webs in the corrugated metal sheets on the ceiling, that no one had been there for a long time, not even Milton's woman, who'd fled just a couple of days after her man disappeared, almost certainly back to her parents' place in Tierra Blanca, or maybe even further, who could say, the fear was catching and *they* had arrived in full force in Progreso, crushing everything in their path. So Polo would skulk around Milton's house then head back outside, past his cousin's old Texan pickup, now covered in dry leaves and flowers from the mango tree that took up that whole side of the property, and finally head down to the little beach overlooking the river to take a seat on the dead tree trunk that Milton used to use as a bench, and Polo would spend hours watching the river's seemingly still waters and the dragonflies skimming across its surface, tossing rocks and chewing tender reeds to curb his craving for a cigarette, for a stiff drink to abate the whirlwind of black thoughts, ethereal yet sharp-edged, that swirled around his head like a blur of moths around a lone light. He would watch the river for a while, chewing on reeds, then take his phone out and use up his credit messaging Milton, to the umpteenth new number, the one he'd given Polo the last time they'd seen each other, weeks earlier, before Polo had even started working at Paradais, and he would sit there waiting for his cousin's reply for a long time, until the sun would finally set and the bright lights of Paradais and the neighbouring luxury developments flickered on, daubing the dun waters in silver, ochre and yellow, less so around the dark strip where the abandoned house stood, scarcely visible behind the branches of the fig tree that stood on the edge of the river and partly concealed the mansion's façade, a filthy, time-ravaged wall with three great misshapen holes in it that to Polo had always looked like the eyes and mouth of a deformed face frozen in a scream or macabre laughter, the laughter of the Bloody Countess, the woman who had ordered the house to be built back in the time of the Spaniards and whom the estuary dwellers had beaten to death for her depraved, diabolical ways, for her habit of snatching boys and young men whom she cherry-picked from among the slaves working her land, subjecting them to unspeakable torture and then finally throwing their remains into a teeming crocodile pit in the mansion's basement. Or at least that's what the old bags in Progreso would say, the same women who swore blind that at night, when the full moon upset the tide and the blue crabs scuttled along the banks of the river, the spectre of the Countess – now an old hag dressed in the rotten rags that had once been her ball gowns, her face stained with her victims' blood – would emerge from the mansion ruins, stretch her arms up to the sky and with spine-chilling wails invoke the forces of evil to protect her, at which point, bathed in a bluish light, she would transform into a mysterious black bird that would fly off into the treetops: a load of bullshit, but bullshit that Polo couldn't help remembering whenever he gazed at the deformed face taunting him from the other side of the river, until at last he would give up waiting and leave the sandy shore before night fell to wander aimlessly around town, which was deserted at that time of evening but for the groups of jumped-up punks, little bums with chocolate milk moustaches whom Polo had no choice but to acknowledge as he passed, tipping his cap so they didn't give him any trouble, so they didn't start any of that shit with their radios and secret codes; pains in the ass who thought they owned the place because they were paid by *them*, and when he could no longer bear the hunger pangs he would make his way home, slip in through the back door and, still on his feet, wolf down the already stale empanadas that Zorayda always left for him on the stove, wrapped in tin foil so the cockroaches couldn't crawl all over them, and he would take a soft drink from the fridge and swig it straight from the bottle, trying not to make a noise so that his mother wouldn't start shouting at him from her bedroom where she was lying on the bed, her hair damp from the shower and wrapped in an old t-shirt that she wound around her head like a turban to avoid getting her pillow wet, the glare from the TV screen dancing across her dour face and Zorayda's body, which would be stretched out on the other bed, her stomach taut, bare, shining with the almond oil that the skank slathered all over herself, the pair of them laughing at some dumb joke or guzzling peanuts or chilli prunes like pigs, with the standing fan positioned right in front of them. Polo would slip past the open door like a ghost and lie down on the petate that stank like a goat, his head resting on one of his grandfather's old shirts and his phone balanced on his bare chest so he'd feel Milton's message vibrate whenever the fucker finally deigned to reply. That was always the first thing he did when he woke up and the last thing he did before going to sleep: look at his phone to check for new messages. Sometimes he even dreamed about Milton; he dreamed he had long conversations with his cousin but he could never remember what they'd said the next morning. Sometimes he dreamed about the haunted mansion and the fig tree that grew on the banks of the river; he dreamed its flowing roots spread out like tentacles to reveal a mansion just like the actual one, just as mouldy and dilapidated only much smaller, like a doll's house where the Bloody Countess's bleeding, still-beating heart lay trapped.

The truth is, had it been up to him, he would never have chosen the zaguan of that godforsaken house for their drinking sessions, and not because he was scared of being in there; he knew all those stories were nonsense, and that the only danger lurking in that crumbling pile were the black widows spinning their webs in its darkest nooks and crannies. No, what got him was the whole vibe of that ruin, the anxiety that seized his body whenever he sat on those big stone steps and how frankly depressing it was to be there in the company of that fat fuckwit while all around them the rain fell, heavy yet invisible, onto the tree canopy suspended above them, a vegetal dome that locked in the damp earth's heat and blocked their view of the river, the sky and Progreso's lights on the opposite bank. It had been Franco's idea, of course, to drink inside that terrible place, when at last he reappeared on the streets of Paradais after days spent hiding away. It turned out he'd been caught completely wasted after their last evening down on the dock, so wasted he'd forgotten his way home and Cenobio had found him passed out and snoring away on one of the poolside sunbeds, much to his grandparents' shame. But not even when they threatened to call his father did Franco tell them who'd got hold of the booze for him, who'd actually bought it; he'd bravely kept his mouth shut while his grandparents roasted him, and eventually, as always, the old couple – who had neither the energy nor the inclination to drag out his punishment – forgave him, and in a matter of days things had gone back to normal, or nearly, because now it was impossible to get any money off them; fatboy's misdemeanour had made them suspicious as hell, and maybe it wasn't such a good idea to go back to the dock now that Cenebio regularly patrolled the area and could catch them. Besides, the evening rains had begun, and who wanted to drink getting soaked in the pissing rain? Maybe they'd be better off finding a new hiding place, the abandoned mansion, for example. They could meet there at nine and wouldn't have to worry about a thing. Who in their right mind would bother them there? Or was Polo too scared? There was something Franco wanted to show him, he'd never guess what, something 'sick', he said, which was enough to convince Polo, who felt a shiver run through him but was also sick of inventing reasons to go into town to fill the endless hours of his evenings, and sick of pretending he didn't miss getting wrecked. And so he turned up at the arranged time and drank thirstily from the heavy square bottle of rum that the lard-ass pulled out of his rucksack, when at last they met again on the front steps of the mansion. They had to drink the rum neat and warm because neither of them had enough money for mixers or ice. Not that they needed it: the rum slid down Polo's throat, sweet, fiery and so delicious, so invigorating that he couldn't stop licking the inside of his mouth after every swig, enthralled by the lingering aftertaste of fruit and caramel that overpowered even the taste of tobacco smoke. For the first time in a hell of a long time he felt blissfully drunk; not pickled or tipsy like usual, but profoundly, melancholically mashed, steeped in a thick stupor that helped him zone out periodically from the stream of shit coming out of fatboy's ass. Because at first Polo thought he'd misheard; no way did that chump have it in him to do what he was claiming he'd done, which was to sneak into the Maroños' house while they were out. Fatboy had known for some time that they never locked the kitchen door, the one leading out into the back yard and the small servant's room where their maid Griselda lived during the week, and one day, with the Maroños away on their cruise, fatboy had snuck into the house. And he'd carried on sneaking in once they were back, on Sundays when his neighbours went out for lunch and spent the afternoon mooching around malls, when the maid made the most of her day off to visit her home town and fatboy was free to drink that smug baldy's home bar dry and then go upstairs to snoop around the master bedroom at leisure and rifle through Señora Marián's drawers and sniff her clothes and her pillow and swipe her panties from the dirty laundry basket in the bathroom. And before Polo could raise his eyebrows in disbelief, fatboy searched inside the pockets of his shorts and pulled out a resealable plastic bag that the animal opened with trembling fingers before reverently extracting a small triangle of black lace. Next, to Polo's astonishment, he held the panties up to his nostrils and sniffed them with a look of pure ecstasy on his face. They still smell, he sighed, and Polo screwed up his face in disgust. Go ahead, have a whiff, Franco offered, and Polo felt like slapping away his outstretched hand. Get the fuck away from me, he muttered, scowling, and fatboy let out a sneering, self-satisfied laugh, an arrogant bray that Polo took as a direct attack against his person, his masculinity.

It was Franco's dumb laugh, plus some Dutch courage from the rum and his generally agitated state, that unleashed Polo's fury. With his lips numb from rage and the booze, Polo opened his mouth and for the first time ever told fatboy what he really thought of him, he and his pathetic little exploit: small time fucking bullshit. Fatboy, who in that precise moment was taking a sip from his plastic cup, coughed nervously. Easy, Polo, what bullshit? he asked, a condescending smile still spread across his chubby face. You think you're so tough, muttered Polo, standing up and flicking the stub he'd been smoking into the darkness. You think you're a big fucking man for breaking into that place and coming out with a fucking pair of baggy old panties, with all the other stuff lying around in that house. Polo poured what was left of the bottle into his plastic cup. Well, I took that bottle you're draining, didn't I? fatboy replied defensively. Not complaining about that, are you? Small time fucking bullshit, Polo repeated, thinking about the jewels that slut draped over herself, the diamond earrings from the party, the silver bangles, the gold rings and her bald cunt of a husband's luxury watches. Polo didn't know shit about designer brands or trends, but he'd bet his own balls that the cheapest of those watches was worth at least his annual gardener's wage; you only had to see the performance that poser put on to check the time, making a real meal of it, just to flash his little toy. Easy, dickhead, fatboy said, leaning over to take the bottle off Polo. You've drained the whole fucking lot, for fuck's sake. Polo downed the contents of his cup. So next time come with, fatboy challenged him, let's see how tough you are. Polo gave him the finger. He stumbled as he bent down to pick up the packet of cigarettes, and when at last he managed to light one, he realized he was alone; fatboy had disappeared. Franco? he called out, without success. The only thing he could hear was the tortured droning of millions of insects and the deafening curtain of rain drawn all around them. Franco, stop fucking around, he shouted, suddenly furious. Had fatboy gone right inside the old mansion? Polo couldn't see a thing from the entrance of the zaguan, just thick darkness flecked with the odd firefly; he may as well have had his eyes closed. Franco? he repeated, and a languorous fart sounded from the darkness followed by a dumb titter that reverberated off the stone walls. I'm having a piss, dickhead, Franco said from somewhere inside. Can't I take a leak in peace? A mourning gecko responded with its unmistakeable chirp and Polo jumped. That's weird, fatboy said, suddenly pensive. It looks like there's a swimming pool in here. Or is it a well? Polo backed away towards the steps. Something pale and gaunt suddenly appeared out of the darkness, dragging itself across the floor: a skeleton hand, Polo thought, its horrible fingers curled like claws. He screamed as he kicked the creature: an enormous crab that had clearly lost its way and which scuttled off towards the nearest trees just as Franco let out a second snigger and yet another fart.

That's the moment Polo began to hate him. But truly hate him, enough to want to break his ugly mug, to smash that square bottle in his face, kick him in the guts and then throw him headfirst into the depths of the river where the treacherous currents would drag his fish-eaten corpse all the way to Alvarado, maybe even further. The shit-eating little poof didn't even have the balls to steal anything worth taking, and with all the valuables lying around in that house, the games consoles and televisions, jewellery and watches, even the cash, for fuck's sake, anything would have been better than that slut's shit-streaked panties.

He couldn't remember how he got home that night. He couldn't even remember waiting for fatboy to come out of the abandoned mansion. When he replayed it in his head the following morning, he saw himself in bursts: images that were disconnected and dreamlike as if shot on a video camera, not seen with his own eyes. He saw himself vomiting copiously against the trunk of an aguacatillo, pedalling into the blinding headlights of the cars on the highway, peeing from the bridge, the stream of urine falling silently into the river's waters, which stank of snatch. If only his traitor of a grandfather had kept his promise to teach him how to build a wooden boat, a simple, reliable craft that he could've upgraded later with a modest motor so he wouldn't have to rely on muscle power alone or be at the mercy of the currents; a dream his grandfather had gradually forgotten with age, and which Polo's mother made damn sure never came to anything when the bitch sold the old man's tools, jumping on the chance as soon as he was bedridden, lost in a world of his own, crying in fear, unable to recognize any of them, unable to understand why they'd tied him to the bed. Polo still hadn't forgiven his mother for that stunt, for having sold his inheritance, the tools that were rightfully his: the handmade saws, the traditional gouges and chisels that his grandfather had fashioned over the years with zero schooling but enough talent to go around, not to mention necessity and hunger. Tools tailored to his swarthy hands, which were rough and disfigured from endlessly chafing against coarse wood and from the countless accidents he had on account of his terrible habit of knocking back rotgut while he worked, and also because the diabetes had shot his nerve endings, which was why he never even felt it if the electric jigsaw – which he had soldered and built himself just by looking at the pictures in a book – would send a chunk of his forefinger flying: just the tip, he would chuckle as he looked around the floor for the missing lump of finger and a rag to soak it in kerosene and light it to cauterize the wound that would be bleeding all over the sawdust-covered floor. He was one tough motherfucker, his grandfather, and completely incomprehensible! Polo had loved him to death, and feared him, too, whenever the old man overdid it on the rotgut and suddenly started talking to himself like a madman and hurling things at the walls! Next to him, Polo felt stupid, clumsy, small, like someone who'd been born yesterday while his grandfather's life stretched back endlessly in time like a really long film in which Polo played a bit part, appearing for a couple of minutes towards the end to deliver some stupid line. His grandfather had never been a kid, that's why he didn't know how to be around them, he'd say. He had worked from the age of six: first as a drover, then as a loader and driver for a furniture company, eventually climbing the ranks there to the position of sales clerk; then as a cook and teacher before doing a stretch inside, and finally, when he came to live in Progreso as a carpenter. And each and every one of those trades he'd learned himself, just watching how it was done, observing and repeating, carving out a living with whatever he had to hand. He also had a string of women across the river basin, in every town where he'd lived, and at least a dozen offspring, some his, some step-children, although the only one he recognized by name was Polo's mother; with her he could be sure, the old bastard would say, that she was his and not some other prick's because she'd been born nine months to the day after a flood that left him and his woman stranded for weeks on the roof of their house, the two of them alone, surrounded by miles of chocolate-brown water; the only daughter of his who looked out for him in his old age and who ended up caring for him at the end, when he was totally gone in the head and couldn't make it to his workshop and would regularly disappear into a world of his own and shuffle into town where he would wander for hours, his hair stiff and wild and his clothes in tatters, white from all the dust on the roads, barefoot or sometimes wearing just one old huarache, its sole fashioned from a piece of car tyre, and Polo wanted to crawl into a hole every time his school friends spotted his grandfather hobble past; they would laugh at the ragged figure he cut and shout things at him while Polo pretended to ignore their insults, until they grew bored of goading the old man and left, at which point Polo would go and pick him up off the ground, from under a shady tree in the square or from the zaguan of some random stranger's house, and try to convince him to come, please, abuelo, people are looking at you, it's your grandson, Polo, let's go home, you don't have to sleep on the floor. But sleeping on the floor had been a habit of his since well before he'd cracked up; at home, Polo's grandfather had always slept on a petate on the living room floor, his huaraches still on his feet and his arms folded under his head to form a pillow, fully dressed no matter how hot it was. Later on, though, he'd fallen ill and stopped recognizing people and only wanted to haunt the streets in town, muttering incoherent thoughts and vulgarities, and they'd had to tie him to the headboard of what, up until then, had been Polo's bed, the twin bed positioned right up against the identical one where his mother slept, the same bed that later Polo would have to give up for Zorayda. His grandfather hated lying on the mattress; you would've thought from the screaming and shouting and the way he thrashed about that the springs were digging into his back, but that wasn't the problem; to Polo it seemed that the problem wasn't so much the mattress as being that close to his daughter, who slept right beside him so she could look after him in the middle of the night. Yes, the old dog believed – and who knows how many times Polo had heard it, given his grandfather's mania for repeating himself – that it was bad for a man's health – 'pernicious', he would say – to sleep so close to a woman; everyone knew that the female humours debilitate, dull the mind, which was why young lads were so feeble and lily-livered, and whenever he said this he would glance at his grandson, his small eyes glinting with derision and disdain, because as a child Polo had never been able to sleep too far from his mother, he simply wouldn't fall asleep if he wasn't nestled into her body and he would scream if ever he woke in the middle of the night and stretched out his hand and she wasn't beside him; and this went on until he was six or seven, when he travelled to Mina with his mother to visit Tia Rosaura and Tia Juanita and some other relatives, none of whom he could remember apart from his cousin Zorayda, six years his elder and always in charge of him while his mother and aunts played cards or went off to the local feria, 'looking for suitors', Polo's mother would say as she applied her lipstick and curled her lashes, her eyes so heavily caked in black make-up they were all but unrecognizable to her son, who would howl, clinging to his mother's leg, inconsolable that she was about to abandon him and, even worse, leave him in the care of evil Zorayda. And his aunts would cry with laughter and call him a scaredy-cat, a big baby, had you ever seen a needier child, they'd say, and his mother had slapped him to calm him down so they could get out of the house and hit the town in their high heels, and Polo carried on crying until Zorayda took him to bed and put her arms around him to calm him down, but he couldn't fall asleep, partly because of the heat, partly because of the horrible feeling in his poor tummy since he'd decided he would hate his mother for the rest of time, and partly because Zorayda wouldn't stop pestering and tickling him: in bed beside him, dressed in nothing but an old t-shirt, that annoying girl would run the tip of her skinny finger up and down Polo's forearm, *this little ant*, she would softly sing as her finger moved higher, all smooth and tingly, *went picking up wood*, zig zagging its way up to his neck, and Polo would shudder, *when out of the sky, the rain poured down*, and bite his lip, because according to Zorayda the whole point of the game was to not laugh, *run home little ant,* not to make a sound, not even when her finger crept towards his belly button or slid under the elastic of his underpants, *or else you'll drown*, or attacked the soft folds of his underarms, his most sensitive area, the one that invariably made him burst out laughing. That contact between them always left him feeling hot and tense and wanting to curl up into Zorayda's body, so different from his own and so different, too, from his mother's: much scrawnier, with jutting bones that dug into him whenever his cousin turned around suddenly and climbed on top of him to torture him and slap him about. There was something diabolical about Zorayda's gaze, a twinkle of knowing vileness that the crafty bitch kept well hidden from the adults, to whom she only ever showed her sweet, obliging side, reserving her tyranny and cruelty for when nobody else was around to stop her. Every night of that awful trip to Mina, whenever they lay down together in that bed, Zorayda would stroke him until he fell into a daze, his skin tingling and

65

his little willy rock hard, but then straight away, for no apparent reason, she would immediately attack him again and pinch his cheeks and poke him with her bony fingers until he cried, her face twisted into an ugly grimace that from one moment to the next could transform into something else entirely: that was his cousin Zorayda's great skill, her astounding facility to transform right before your eyes and project whichever image people wanted from her: Zorayda, sweet and obedient with her plaits hanging down at her waist, wearing the batiste dresses that Tia Rosaura made for her; Zorayda, solemn and diligent for her employees as a housemaid in Mina; Zorayda, stupid and defenceless for Polo's mother, deceived by a bad man and abandoned with his child; or Zorayda the crazy bitch who would do anything to fuck Polo, for the sheer pleasure of ruining his life, because he'd never asked for it, he'd never given her any ideas; he barely ever looked at her, he hated that two-faced little parasite. On the face of it she'd come to Progreso to help Polo's mother with his grandfather, but instead she spent all her time making excuses to go down to Doña Pacha's store to flirt with the delivery guys, and Polo's mother never said a thing or gave her the grief she gave him every day, like how the hell did Polo still not have a job when they could barely rub two beans together, who the hell did that lazy sack of shit think he was, a big man when he was out on the sauce, picking his belly button fluff, but not so much when it came to finding work. As if it were that easy, Christ! he'd want to tell her. As if fucking jobs grew on trees! Where exactly was he supposed to pull a job out of? And doing what, for God's sake, and where? Nobody wanted to hire him, for all the early starts he made to fill in the stupid fucking applications his mother brought home, writing in the little boxes with his tiny scrawl, all in capital letters, over and over the same fucking information: first name, father's last name, mother's last name, education, health, life goal. What did they need to know all that for, what the fuck was it to them? And what the fuck was that 'life goal' business? He always left that part blank because he had no fucking clue what to put down. Once he'd filled the applications in, he'd then have to head in to Boca to deliver them, but not before ducking into the yard to have a quick wash in the drum of water, patting himself dry, throwing on some talc and getting dressed in the one pair of smart trousers he owned, the scuffed shoes he used to wear to school and any t-shirt he could find without holes in it, and then he'd cross the dirt road and take the bus to Boca, carrying his shitty fucking applications to the stores that were looking for young men, school leavers, ready to put the hours in. But he always returned to Progreso empty-handed, with nothing to show for his efforts, forced to put up with his pain-in-the-ass cousin, who, under the pretext of taking care of the house, would spend all day winding him up, muttering innuendos and wiggling her ass, leaning into him when she cleared his plate, or 'accidentally' brushing past him when they met in the hallway, squeezing his arm for no reason at all and commenting, with mock surprise, on how strong he'd got, how much he'd filled out, who would have thought a skinny runt like him would grow into such a well-hung stud, and she would flash him a dirty grin, her eyes wandering down to that part of Polo's anatomy, which invariably became swollen and stiff, taking him back to that trip to Mina, to the guilt and rage he thought he'd erased from his memory through the sheer will to forget it, in the same way he'd forgotten about the tantrums he used to throw on his mother, how he'd wimpishly latch on to her to fall sleep. It had all come flooding back the moment Zorayda turned up in Progreso, supposedly to help Polo's mother with his grandfather, although underneath it all it seemed more like the girl had come on holiday, because there wasn't a day she didn't swan off for a splash in the river with some neighbour, not an evening she didn't go loitering around the store, chatting to the traders and the delivery truck drivers, or to anyone with a dick between his legs that she could rub herself against like a cat. That is some desperate pussy, Milton would say whenever Zorayda showed up at the store to snoop and get the latest gossip, while he and Polo drank beer out the back. She'll start blowing bubbles from her gash soon, Milton would say to wind him up, but Polo never took it to heart: they'd been best friends their whole lives, cousins – or almost, because Polo's grandfather had brought up Milton's dad as if he were one of his own, before Polo's mother was even born – and Polo didn't get wound up when Milton said those things about his cousin – which were true in any case – or when Milton gave him advice about how to dress or introduce himself when it came to finding work, little tricks to gain the employers' trust so they didn't take him for a fucking crook or the village idiot. Polo would hear him out but he never saw the point in wearing hair gel or giving a firm handshake. Milton couldn't see that a new hairstyle or wearing deodorant was never going to fix Polo's trouble finding a job; it was all right for him: the lucky prick was half *güero*, as pale as a ghost even under the fierce coastal sun, with thick dreamy lashes and that mop of wavy hair he was always flicking off his forehead like some soap opera stud, while Polo, well, Polo was *prieto*, there was no other way to put it, dark skinned and ugly as sin, his mother would say – and she would know, since they were identical – and he'd been born with a grim sort of gaze that instantly gave him away as someone lacking a life goal. But Milton insisted that none of that mattered, and when it came down to it the only thing that mattered was his attitude, Polo only needed to roll his sleeves up and put a little effort in, let's talk over a beer somewhere, *papi*, and he would lend Polo cash to buy credit for his phone, give him a ride home whenever he got shitfaced, and promise him that if Polo really couldn't find any work he would speak to his broth-er-in-law, see if they could give him a gig helping out at the scrapyard, but all that went down the drain on that Friday during carnival when *they* abducted Milton out-side his house on his way back from one of his trips to the southern border with his brother-in-law, and Polo didn't hear from him until three months later when they finally let his cousin make a quick stop in Progreso to sort out his personal affairs, of which, truth be told, he didn't have many because Milton's woman was long gone, back living with her family in Tierra Blanca. She didn't want to know a thing about him or whatever the fuck had gone on, and nor was Milton keen to tell her and drag her into it, so he spent his one free day with Polo, just like the old times, but instead of passing caguamas back and forth out the back of Doña Pacha's store, they went for tacos in some fancy joint in Boca, on the banks of the river, like two head honchos, and Milton told Polo the short version of what had happened the night they abducted him and his brother-in-law, while Polo listened and stuffed himself with tacos al pastor and beer. Milton, on the other hand, just chain-smoked cigarette after cigarette and kept sniff-ing as if he were snorting coke on the sly even though he swore to Polo that he wasn't, he wasn't into that shit, and all the while their waiter threw glances at the bulge of Milton's gun at his hip and made out like he wasn't listen-ing to a thing Polo's cousin was saying.

This is how it'd gone down: on that Friday in February, Milton was making his way home at about two in the morning and was on his knees, so braindead from the eighteen hours he'd driven from Chiapas he didn't even spot *them* waiting for him outside his house: a great big pickup full of fuckers he'd never set eyes on in his life, and Milton didn't even put up a fight, nor did he have the strength to make a run for it because he'd been driving nonstop for fucking hours and he was on one of those speed comedowns where you feel like you're about to have heart attack, and to make matters worse, those assholes were armed, so what the fuck could he do. They wrestled him into the pickup, took everything he had on him – his wallet, his keys and his phone – threw him on the floor so no one could see him, his head bleeding, and drove around in circles for hours so he couldn't figure out where they were going, even though Milton guessed they were somewhere around the wetlands, near the airport from the sound of the low-flying planes. Anyway, after a few hours of driving him here and there like a prick, they let him out on some kind of ranch, led him inside a house, locked him in a room and beat a confession out of him, forcing him to tell them what the story was at the border, who owned the car business, who they were working with, and at first Milton had held it together, but when they started with the electric shocks he caved and spilled his guts, he couldn't take the pain, he even pissed himself, and the most fucked up thing of all was that in the next door room they were doing the same thing to some other fucker, and Milton could hear the guy crying like a bitch. He figured it was his brother-in-law they had in there but he couldn't make out his voice from the moaning and howling, and Milton wasn't about to ask if it was him, if it really was his brother-in-law: he was giving nothing away, but in the end, when they started shocking him, he told them everything, absolutely everything, because the pain was unbearable and they'd already started cutting the guy in the next door room. Milton couldn't see a thing, his head was inside a sack that smelled of pure shit, but those assholes beating him senseless gave him a running commentary: now they were cutting off the guy next door's ears because he wouldn't cooperate, now his fingers, now his hands, and finally they cut off his head, judging from the bloodcurdling sounds, and that's why Milton ended up telling them everything they wanted to know about his brother-in-law's business: numbers, takings, the names of the people working with them, their contacts in the state police department, their preferred routes across the border, and even their tricks for forging licence plates, he told them everything, and by the time he was done blabbing, instead of putting him down like an animal, as Milton thought they would, they left him in peace until daybreak when one of those assholes came to wake him up, removed the sack from his head and gave him a drink of water, at which point Milton could see that he was in a cement block room with a corrugated metal roof and that standing in front of him was a young woman with light brown hair, dressed in jeans, a shirt and sunglasses. She looked around twenty, twenty-five tops, but she seemed to be the boss of all those assholes because even the beefiest motherfuckers among them stood to attention before her and remained bolt upright looking ahead when the woman ran her eyes over them, and they spoke to her in the formal *usted* and as *licenciada*, although it was hard to believe she was a graduate from the way she spoke, rough and gruff like a *ranchera*, and Milton immediately understood that there was no fucking around with this woman, so when she started laying down the law Milton just stared at the floor, at her cowboy boots, and answered yes to everything she said, yes, señora, yes, *licenciada*, while she went on: we'll give you a chance 'cos we know you know the business, but if you don't want the work you're well within your rights, it's just that we know where you live now, where your whole family lives, we know who your partner is and what she does, and the truth is Milton didn't even think about it, he agreed immediately: he even had the good sense to thank her, to come across as genuinely grateful, even though inside he was shitting himself because the woman said they'd give him one shot, just one, that's what she said, and only because they were in a hurry to get the scrapyard business up and running, but if he fucked up, even once, she'd finish him off, him and his woman, their families and even their neighbours, and Milton just kept saying yes to everything, yes he understood, yes it was all good.

The next thing, the woman ordered his release and told her men to get him washed up and to give him some clothes to go out in and to sew up the gash on his head before taking him, right away, to see if he was up to the job or if it made more sense after all to finish him off. So they put Milton in another poky room and left him to wash and put on some clean clothes, brand new clothes, straight out of the pack, at which point a harried little lady – round as a ball and with a face like a slapped ass – rushed in and barked at him to sit down on an upturned bucket so she could sew him up. After that, someone else came in and handed him a baseball cap to cover the stiches and he was led to a room at the front of the house where the same little lady who had hurriedly stitched him up was now standing at an enormous pan of burning oil frying garnachas while a dozen men, almost all of them young guys, ate in silence at plastic tables, their eyes raised to watch the game on the wall-mounted TV – América versus Nexaca, he could still remember – drinking cans of soft drink which they took from an old fridge rattling away in the corner. It looked like any other *fonda*, like any other cheap shack in the middle of nowhere, and they sat him down beside a quiet, dark-skinned kid, eating garnachas from the plate the pit bull had put in front of him, and who didn't say a word to Milton or to anyone else for that matter, didn't explain what was going on or what would happen next. He later learned the guy went by the name of El Gritón, Gasbag, because he almost never opened his mouth (but that was later); by this point Milton still didn't have a fucking clue what was going on and he was just trying to guess where the next blows would come raining down from, and he sat peering out of the open door that led onto the street, or rather onto a deserted path in the middle of nowhere, wondering how far he could get before those assholes popped a cap in his ass.

Once El Gritón had finished eating, he elbowed Milton and motioned at him to get up and follow him. Outside the *fonda*, Milton realized that it was no ranch but a cement block building slapped in the middle of a deserted highway, surrounded by mangos and undergrowth and little else. Standing on the edge of the road was another guy, also very young and very dark, freshly showered and dressed in a shirt and pressed trousers, even wearing aftershave. The guy introduced himself as El Sapo, The Toad, then he handed Milton the first cigarette he'd smoked in days. The smoke was just going to Milton's head when the next thing he knew he was in a double-cab pickup with the others headed to Veracruz and the Cuauhtémoc IMSS building. Neither El Sapo nor El Gritón nor the driver gave him any explanation, and Milton was too scared shitless to ask so he just went along with it and did as they did, which was to walk into a snack bar in front of the hospital, order a torta milanesa and a carton of guayaba-flavoured Boing and scarf down both even though they'd only just eaten back at the fonda, like bottomless waste grinders. After that they just hung out for a while smoking and watching the cars go by on the street outside, until finally El Gritón gave El Sapo a signal and all three of them left the snack bar and hailed a taxi and El Sapo peeped his head through the open window to ask the driver how much he'd charge to take them to the Bodega Aurrerá megastore in Puente Moreno. Milton didn't catch the driver's reply, he simply climbed into the back seat when El Sapo opened the front passenger door, and they drove off. El Sapo rode up front beside the driver, and behind him was El Gritón, with Milton next to him. A few streets further along, El Sapo struck up some small talk with the old timer driving the taxi, how about this heat, eh, you see the Tiburones game?, would you take a look at that ass, and having broached the topic of asses, the taxi driver – a grubby, scruffy old fuck wearing a wife beater vest with his stinking hairy pits on show – perked up and began telling them about all the women he'd fucked, he even gave the three of them tips on how to keep a woman in line, how to mould her to their liking, and El Sapo and El Gritón were laughing their heads off at the bullshit that reeking old fart was spewing, and Milton tried his best to laugh too, to act normal, because even though nobody told him what to do, he figured that that was the attitude he should assume. Anyway, El Sapo didn't stop ribbing the wrinkly prick for the whole journey, until finally they reached the Aurrerá car park and the old man pulled up and told El Sapo, let's call it a round hundred, and El Gritón protested from the back, the first time Milton had heard him speak: a hundred pesos my ass, and at that point Milton noticed he had a cable in his hands, a thin steel cable that he lifted over the seat to strangle the taxi driver, but the old man managed to slip his hand between the cable and his neck and that's when El Sapo pulled the handbrake and held a gun to his head. Easy, easy, take the money, the taxi driver said. You think I give a fuck about your fucking money? El Gritón replied, right in his ear, you're fuckin' dead, you limpdick fuckin' lowlife. Milton was so confused he didn't notice the reinforcements arrive: two kids who drove up out of nowhere, stopped beside the taxi and started opening the doors. One of them launched on top of the driver and, together with El Sapo, started shouting and laying into him before pulling him out of the taxi and throwing him into the boot. At the same time, the other guy opened Milton's door and, with no warning at all, shoved him over so that he could climb in next to him. El Sapo got behind the wheel, fixed the rear-view mirror, smoothed his gelled hair and released the handbrake and they flew out of the car park without anyone saying a word, as if nothing had happened.

They drove to the neighbourhoods near the water treatment plant where they pulled some shit so crazy it took a while for Milton to work out what was even going on: they cruised around in the taxi until they saw a delivery guy on a motorbike, who they'd start tailing, and, just as they were getting really close, El Sapo would step on the gas and knock him over, gauging it right so that the drivers went flying but their bikes were left with as little damage as possible; with the delivery guy on the ground, sometimes scraped to shit, El Gritón and the other two would jump out of the car and kick the shit out of him at gunpoint, then one of them would hastily check over the bike, climb on and race out of there, at which point the rest of them would climb back into the taxi to hunt for more delivery guys in the next neighbourhood, and this happened three times, until there was no one left in the taxi but El Sapo at the wheel and Milton in the backseat, confused as hell because no one had bothered to explain how it all worked, but El Sapo was in no mood for lick-ass questions, so Milton kept his trap shut.

El Sapo sped off towards Tejería and turned down a desolate dirt track. For miles and miles, as far as the eye could see, there was nothing there but thick, low-lying undergrowth and the odd bony, hollow-eyed cow. The dirt road was steadily narrowing and eventually they reached a point where it was impossible to keep going because the undergrowth surrounded them on all sides. At that point, El Sapo stopped the car, looked at Milton through the rear-view mirror and told him to look live-ly, it was time; El Sapo ordered him to get out of the car and help him open the boot, from which they hauled the reeking taxi driver whose hands were tied behind his back with plastic cable ties, preventing him from getting up by himself. The sad old fucker wasn't so cocky now: his mop of wet, tangled hair was sticking to his sweaty face, he'd pissed himself and was sobbing, begging for his life, for them not to kill him, please, have mercy, in the name of the Holy Virgin, gentlemen, please. El Sapo kicked him a couple of times on the ground; with a look of disgust he wiped his hands on his trouser legs and finally pulled out his piece from his waistband; with his left hand he took out another, smaller gun that he'd been wearing at the small of his back, and he passed it to Milton, who took it, still not sure what the fuck was going on. Flick the safety off, El Sapo said, and he patiently explained to Milton how. He seemed pretty relaxed, almost friendly. Then you cock the gun like this and wipe the fucker out, he said, gesturing towards the old man. Milton's balls had shrunk to the size of peanuts, but he knew the time had finally come, the time to prove he was cut out for the job, and that if he pussied out El Sapo would waste him in a second, so his only two options were to pop the old fucker and keep *them* happy, or to pop El Sapo before he could read his mind, bolt like an animal into the wild and face the consequences, but El Sapo just shook his head at him and smirked as if to say 'I wouldn't if I were you' and he pointed his gun at Milton and shook it impatiently: come on, for fuck's sake, I don't have time for this, it's late, and Milton raised his gun and aimed it at the reeking, snivelling old taxi driver who was writhing around on the sand. He guessed he should shoot him in the head, but he couldn't get close enough, and El Sapo didn't tell him what to do, he didn't give him any more advice, he just stood there aiming at Milton with his own piece, his eyebrows raised expectantly. The old man had his face to the ground and was praying: *Dios te salve, reina y madre de misericordia.* And in his head Milton responded: *Vida, dulzura y esperanza nuestra,* and right there and then he knew that if that old man got to the end of the prayer, he wouldn't be able to kill him, and El Sapo would have to finish off the pair of them, and so he clenched his ass, clamped his mouth and eyelids shut and fired, landing a shot in the old man's back and filling the air with the terrified squawking and flapping of hundreds of little black birds which had been hiding in the surrounding undergrowth. El Sapo had to shout to make himself heard over the racket of the birds and the man's screams: finish him, he was saying, shoot him in the head, and Milton squeezed the trigger twice more but both times failed to hit the old fuck, even though he was barely moving now, until finally, on the third try, he managed to land a bullet in his cheek and the taxi driver was put out of his misery and they could get the hell out of there.

From there they headed back to base, to the *fonda* where the grumpy little lady was still slaving away frying garnachas in her giant pan and the same posse of assholes was sitting around plastic tables eating. The heat emanating from the bubbling pan of boiling oil and the tin roof was unbearable. They stayed there for a while until El Gritón and the other two assholes from before drove up on the stolen motorbikes, parked them in a kind of courtyard behind the quarters and then entered the *fonda* whooping and laughing, yakking like a pair of pumped teenagers, and even El Gritón had a smile on his face. Milton didn't dare ask what it was all about, but when the local news came on the wall-mounted TV, the headline story was a series of coordinated attacks at five petrol stations in the Boca del Río region that had taken place that very afternoon, just hours earlier, and the guys from the *fonda* made such a commotion that Milton could no longer hear what the newsreader was saying, just something about how the criminals had been driving motorbikes and were armed, and on a news ticker across the bottom of the screen he read that those armed robbers had stolen over half a million pesos in under an hour. The gang was euphoric and more than ready for a drink, but the same crank from before put them in their place when they ordered her to get the beers out, she told them not to be fucking stupid, they had to wait for the *licenciada* to authorize it, and she went back to frying her garnachas, completely deaf to the men's pleas and insults. Milton wasn't sure what happened after that: he was suddenly overwhelmed with tiredness and he fell fast asleep right there at the plastic table until a dude shook him and led him to a bed in one of the bunkhouses at the back, where the screams of people being tortured mingled with the moans from the dirty videos some ass-holes were watching on the next bunk along; Milton couldn't get back to sleep, he just lay there as the salsa verde he'd eaten with his garnachas repeated on him, his wide eyes gaping at the ceiling even though they were stinging from the shattering eighteen-hour drive from Tapachula plus the other thirty-something hours of beatings he'd endured at the back of that very building. Each time he tried to close his eyes and sleep, Milton would see that reeking old taxi driver's snivelling face, even hear his prayers to God, at which point Milton would open his eyes again and replay every minute that had passed since they'd kicked him into that pickup outside his house, to convince himself that he'd had no choice, that it had been his life or that wrinkly fuck's; the life of his woman and their entire families, or the life of that old fart who'd lived the best part of his anyway. And ever since then he hadn't been able to sleep, he told Polo. Instead, every two or three days, his body would collapse and he'd black out for a while. That was what falling asleep felt like now, but the truth was that not even then could he avoid the nightmares, and he noticed the same was true for a lot of the boys: they would moan and cry and even talk in their sleep, and there was always one weirdo who'd kick off out of nowhere, start ranting and raving just because someone was snoring or farted; although, of course, the scariest of them all were the ones who slept like angels the moment their heads hit their mattresses, they really were sketchy motherfuckers.

When he finished telling the story of his abduction, Milton fell silent; after another two or three cigarettes, he told Polo it was time he got going and that he'd give him a lift back to Progreso. They walked out of the taco joint and the waiter at the door ran to get the car: a massive pickup with a hulking bonnet that roared when Milton put his foot on the accelerator, halogen headlights that startled the stray dogs, and a suspension that glided effortlessly over the filthy water-logged potholes on the road into town. The only thing that took the shine off that monster truck was the dry mud spattered all over the black bodywork, layer upon layer of encrusted mud and grass that was crying out for a good scrub, but that didn't seem to bother Milton, and neither did the grungy cabin interior, the dirty, ragged upholstery, the floor covered in crushed cigarette butts, grime and empty bottles. Best whisky in the world, Milton had said, liquid fuckin' gold, *papi*, when Polo picked up a bottle from the floor and looked at the label written in English, the old thirst tickling his throat again, firing the faint throbbing in his head. His cousin had agreed to buy him some beers from the store but he refused to get out the coke; he said he didn't have any on him, that he wasn't into that shit, and Polo suspected he was lying so he didn't have to share it and that, once again, Milton was treating him like a dumb little kid, because Milton was definitely buzzing, jumpy, constantly sniffling and pastier than ever, his dreamy eyes sunken behind big cartoon bulldog dark circles, his teeth nicotine-yellow from the chain smoking, which he kept up even as he drove, as though he could only breathe if through those golden filters.

Polo would have liked Milton to turn off the air con and roll down the tinted windows, not only because the locked-in smoke was making his eyes sting and the icy air had given him goosebumps, but so that those lowlife squeakers strutting around the plaza could see him out with his cousin and show a little respect, but Milton didn't even respond when Polo asked if he could turn down the air con. He was driving straight towards the river, towards his house, or what had once been his house, his mind elsewhere, and when they arrived, he parked under the mango tree like in the old days but he didn't want to get out. What for? he asked Polo. What was the point? His woman – his *ex*, he should say – didn't want anything to do with him, and maybe it was better that way, maybe everything had happened for a reason, he said, and Polo didn't know what to say. He got the feeling that the guy sitting behind the wheel smoking beside him wasn't his cousin, that he was no longer the same Milton – cheerful and carefree, foul-mouthed and optimistic – but a different person entirely, one who looked like the old Milton, but wasn't him. For a start, his cousin – practically his brother – would never have preached to him like that, like some dreary constipated priest. The real Milton never spoke to Polo as if he was, what, his big brother? His *father*? Don't give in to temptation, he cautioned him that night, don't let ambition run away with you, because the second you get into this shit, there's no turning back; don't be like those stupid punks who think they're big fucking bosses with their motorbikes and their radios when they don't have the first fuckin' clue about what they're wrapped up in. Sermons that went on and on while Polo just nodded steadily, lightheaded from trying to keep up with the demented pace of his cousin's smoking, his stomach like a pot of rage bubbling away in painful silence, his arms twitchy from the urge to open his door and get the fuck out of there so he didn't have to listen to the horseshit coming from that fucking hypocrite Milton's mouth, telling him there was nothing like an honest job! Meanwhile he cruised around in that luxury pickup with three brand-new cellphones clipped to his belt and a wallet full of five hundred-peso notes that Polo had clocked when Milton picked up the tab for the beers and tacos. He had a fucking nerve! Of course Polo didn't want to be a squeaker, he didn't want anything to do with those small-time snoops, always standing on the same corner of the plaza; cheap, disposable pawns. He was destined for better, more sophisticated things, and it was obvious he had the balls Milton lacked. What was so wrong with wanting to earn some real money, wanting to be free and to have a sense of worth, of purpose, the closest thing to a life goal Polo had ever felt? Milton was stupid enough to think Polo's silence meant he was impressed by the things he said, when really it was the unbearable sadness of having lost his cousin – his best and only friend – for good. That guy talking to him now, lecturing him and pushing money on him out of pity, wasn't his oldest buddy, he was someone else entirely, some other cunt who, incidentally, wouldn't last two minutes working for *them* because he was too soft, too nice, he overthought everything and he'd be a dead man before long. So even though Polo was dying to get that business with Zorayda off his chest, in the end he said goodbye to Milton without telling him any of his own problems, and besides, he was sure, completely sure, or almost completely sure, that he had nothing to do with Zorayda's condition; everyone knew his cousin was a goer, right? Or at least that's what people in town said about her, that she spread her legs for any guy who asked, and that's why the kid she was expecting could be anyone's in town, anyone's, and besides, he hadn't even come inside her, not once, he'd swear on his grandfather's grave; not even the first time had he given himself the pleasure of dumping his load inside her, the day he finally had enough of her touchy-feely bullshit, her crass insinuations, her my, haven't you grown, Polo, do you remember the games we used to play? and that day, when they were alone in the

82

house, Polo couldn't contain his hatred for that fucking bitch a second longer and he pushed her up against the back of the armchair, yanked down her hotpants and rammed his rock hard cock inside her while the little whore panted and slapped her hand on the back of the chair without a clue of what was going on. It was the worst mistake of his life, the worst fucking mistake of his lousy miserable life because instead of settling matters, after that, the horny bitch wouldn't leave him in peace; he'd meant to humiliate her, to hurt her, but the little hoe had got a taste for Polo roughing her up and wanted to milk him like a cow every five seconds, and she'd follow him around the house begging him to give it to her, to fill her up, running her sneaky hands up Polo's arms and shoulders, *this little ant*, across his chest and stomach, *went picking up wood*, until he'd explode and pin down her arms and force himself inside her, pounding and pounding away, finally coming on her ass or her brown stomach, or on the hard living room floor, but never giving her the cum she asked for open mouthed. Every time he screwed Zorayda he promised himself he wouldn't do it again: that was the last time he'd fuck her, the last time he'd be taken in by that ass, which he knew would only land him in trouble, give him some kind of rank disease, or worse. Every single time he pulled out of her wet cunt, which reeked of river sludge, and ejaculated liberally into his own hand, he swore to himself that it wouldn't happen again, no matter what the crafty bitch said to him with those eyes of hers, the eyes of a cat in heat, no matter how good it felt when she rubbed him through his clothes or how hard he got when she ran her tongue over it; but despite his own promises, when he least expected it, there he'd be again, screwing her, driving his cock all the way in, punishing her, while he told himself, in despair, that this really was the last time he'd screw her, the last time he'd fuck her, this time he really meant it, before coming on the floor and pulling up his trousers and running out of the house, dishevelled and sweaty and stinking of rotten fish, with his botched job applications in his hand, ready to beg for a job, any job, it didn't matter, any fucking job so long as it got him out of Progreso. That was his life goal. Not to 'better himself', as his stupid mother had insisted when Polo asked her what the fuck he was supposed to write in that box. 'Better yourself', what a load of shit, what the fuck was it even supposed to mean? Race against yourself? Against an identical twin you wouldn't think twice about tripping up and leaving in the dust? No, his life goal was to get the fuck out of there, earn some cash, be free, goddammit, free for once in his fucking life, and that asshole Milton didn't want to help him. That asshole Milton had switched sides, he'd sided with Polo's mother who had agreed to let Zorayda stay with them and have her kid because it was the right thing to do, the proper thing, and even though initially she'd flipped her lid when the girl confessed she was pregnant, they ended up in each other's arms, making plans, sharing the pain and strife of being a single mother, what fault did the little ones have, you had to find a way to provide for them, and Polo watched the pair of them from the door, frozen, dumbstruck with terror, unable to get his head around any of it, and later he would try to speak to his mother in private, to make her see sense and convince her it would be better for everyone if they sent his cousin back to Mina with the aunts, let them sort out the girl's mistake, because why should Polo and his mother pay the price for her whoring around, when everyone in town knew that the little skank put it about left, right and centre, with the street vendors and the drinks delivery guys and the drivers who stopped by Doña Pacha's store; he didn't know for sure that she'd slept with all of them, but surely she had, right? It had to be true, if everyone in town said so. But his mother cut him short, she didn't even let him finish his point that anyone in town could have fathered that kid, instead shutting him up with a short, sharp slap in the face and barking at him, who the hell did he think he was, telling her what to do? How dare that stupid boy lay down the law in her house? He couldn't even get a proper job, or any fucking job for that matter, because he was a dropout and a drunk like his grandfather, but at least his grandfather had worked from dusk till dawn every single day all his life, and thanks to all that toil, all that sweat, blood and tears he'd managed to provide for them, not like that dropout Polo, living in fantasy land. Who the fuck did he think he was? And she'd given him a couple more smacks before sending him to sleep on the living room floor. And one morning, two or three days after that fight, she woke him up at the crack of dawn and, practically dragging him by the scruff, led him to the offices of the Gulf Real Estate Company where that cocksucker Urquiza had the contract ready and waiting for Polo to sign and sell his soul for a measly wage that in any case got snaffled by his mother, who was overjoyed, of course, because with his wages she could finally make ends meet and there was enough to cover the numerous debts and small loan payments she'd been forced to defer. And Zorayda's horrible belly kept growing and growing, and Polo had no choice but to come home as late as possible and dead drunk to avoid meeting his cousin's gaze, with her sneaky cat eyes that flashed with a new glint of satisfaction and boldness as she smeared her belly in almond oil. The bitch would laugh at him whenever Polo's mother wasn't looking, and when their eyes met for even a second she would smile and throw him a complicit wink, relishing holding all the cards and having absolute power to destroy Polo's life if he dared try to challenge her: the slightest show of disrespect or rudeness, the first sign of a hand being raised to her and she would run and tell Polo's mother everything, because if she was going down, he was going with her, that's how this works, cuz: you carry on working and bringing home the bacon, that's what men are for, right? That's what Zorayda's eyes seemed to say, and no amount of effort, not even the filthiest bender with fatboy, could change that or halt the growth of her fucking horrifying gut, or fully dispel the anguish, the crushing feeling in Polo's each morning, the knot of anxiety that would get lodged in his throat as soon as he heard the shrill tinkling of the phone's alarm clock from the bedroom, which he had to immediately obey if he didn't want his mother to come down on him, screaming and coming at him with her flip flop; his eyes would still be glued together with sleep as he shuffled out into the yard wearing only his pants and went over to the giant drum they filled each day with water from the well to wash the dishes and their clothes and to flush the toilet, and placed his hands on the rusty rim and took a deep breath as he plunged his head all the way down to his shoulders into the cool water, as if that drum were the opening to a natural pool of crystal clear water that Polo could dive into, swimming right to the bottom and out the other side.

In the beginning he thought it was just talk, more of Franco Andrade's fucked-up fantasies, more shit spewing from that lecherous twat's mouth because he didn't have the slightest clue what he was talking about. It was so obvious the prick had never been with a woman, had never put his flaccid little dick anywhere near a pussy, which is why he was so obsessed with boning the one bitch who'd smile and talk to him without wincing at the sight of his love handles and repugnant teenage spots. The slut must have known the kid was crazy about her, that he only ever went to their house to lech over her, running back to his room later to rub one out, and maybe it even amused her to turn the idiot on, maybe she got a kick out of it too and liked the attention, enjoyed being desired by that lard ass who could no longer think of anything but boning her. And it wasn't like the woman wasn't hot; there were photos to prove it, she was always in those gossip magazines the *doñas* in Paradais loved so much. She still had it, and any red-blooded male would be more than happy to bend her over and give her a seeing to, right? But fatboy's obsession went way beyond having the horn. Who knew what treasures or marvels he expected to find up that snatch; who knew what he thought would happen when he did finally stick his cock inside her. Sometimes Polo felt like telling him it wasn't such a big deal. Yeah, it felt good; yeah, you forgot about everything when you were pumping away, you felt like the baddest motherfucker on the planet, but that feeling never lasted long enough and sooner or later you had to pull out and deal with all the other stuff, all the whining and sneaky shit from the woman you'd just screwed. Fatboy would be better off just hiring a whore, some tender lovin' woman who looked like his neighbour and would be more than happy to pop his cherry for a modest sum. But no. Fatboy didn't want to plough any old bitch; he wanted Señora Marián de Maroño and it was he who reached the conclusion that he'd have to do it by force, and before his grandparents shunted him off to Puebla to the military academy where they planned to transfer him the second the summer holidays were over.

Once again they were back inside the mansion ruins, sitting on the steps in the covered entrance hall, this time getting pissed on caña diluted in large cartons of orange juice because they were totally broke. As always, Polo had his eyes on the zaguan's interior where the undergrowth and bindweed formed a miniature forest full with fireflies and what sounded like a strident army of cicadas. The caña had gone to his head and was making the insects glow brighter still, filling his eyeline with blinding speckles that every so often dazzled him and made his heart race. He knew there was nothing inside those ruins, nothing that could really hurt them, but he could feel the traces of some ancient, underground current that made him sweat profusely, jiggle his leg up and down and shudder each time the thunder rumbled in the distance, all while pretending to listen to fatboy ramble on about his most recent raid on the Maroños' house. Did Polo know Señora Marián kept toys, sex toys, at the back of a drawer in her wardrobe? he was saying with a shit-eating grin and wiping away drool with the back of his hand while Polo asked himself once again what the fuck he was doing there, why the fuck he didn't just get up and leave. What was the point in being anywhere anymore when everything worked against him anyway, and was due to get worse, and not even half a litre of caña could drown the miserable thought of the baby floating at that very moment in the murky, yellowish fluid filling Zorayda's revolting stomach. What would happen in a few months when that thing was born? What would Polo do if his skanky cousin tried to rope him in to her mess and saddle him with that kid who, as far as he knew, could be pretty much anyone's in town? How would he ever convince his mother it was all their fault: his mother's for having allowed that oversexed pervert, that predacious spider into the house against Polo's will; and Zorayda's above all for throwing herself at him whenever they were alone, baiting him with her stupid little games, with her nasty ways? He had to get out of there before the shit hit the fan. But how? With what money? If he had the chance to go inside the Maroños' house like fatboy did, he wouldn't waste it looking at panties and old photos of Señora Marián as a little girl, no way. He'd clean out the jewellery and watches, the consoles and flat screens, and then fly out of there to find Milton. What's more, if he knew how to drive like that fat prick did, he'd take the white Grand Cherokee too and head straight to Milton's brother-in-law's scrapyard – the one that now belonged to *them* – and he'd hand it straight over, no strings attached, a goodwill gesture to earn their trust, to show them he was ready to roll his sleeves up and get his hands dirty, to do anything they asked, and Milton would vouch for him, tell them he was on a level, and even that miserable bitch, the so-called *licenciada*, would be impressed and give him a chance to prove himself on the job, and he'd never have to set foot in his house or Progreso again.

He'd smiled at that thought, only to look up to see fatboy also smiling, having just muttered some shit Polo hadn't heard, but then something – something he couldn't put his finger on, almost like a deep current, a pulsating, living thing that had no name – united them momentarily in the darkness of that archway creeping with vines. What would you do? fatboy asked him, his voice clear and shrill like a little girl's. How would you convince her? Polo immediately thought of Zorayda's ass, of his cousin's round, brown ass pressed up against his groin while he imagined he was raping her, and he shrugged his shoulders. She'll never fuck you out of choice, he said. She thinks you're a loser, she'd eat you for breakfast. Maybe it's not a question of convincing her, right? Franco went on, having thought for a second. Maybe it's a question of making her, he said. Oh yeah, Polo blurted out, and doing time with a string of juvies lined up to ass-fuck you. You know what they do to rapists in jail, don't you? An eye for an eye, an ass for an ass. But I'm a minor, Franco said, and my dad's a lawyer, a top fucking lawyer, he'd never let them lock me up, that's for no-hopers, as he says. Your old man can have all the contacts he likes, Polo replied, he can pay off all the people he wants, but can't you see her husband's on the TV? You really think Maroño doesn't have his own favours to call in? That he'll just sit there twiddling his thumbs while he watches you bone his wife? Maybe if no one finds out it was me, fatboy proposed, and Polo burst out laughing. Are you fucking kidding me, he said, choking on his cigarette smoke, there's literally no mistaking you: fat, pasty, squeaky-ass voice. Franco didn't respond, but nor did he wipe the obscene smile from his face, that row of big white straight teeth that, in the flickering torchlight, looked like the smile of an annoying magical cat Polo had once seen in a cartoon. If I kill her after, she won't be able to tell anyone it was me, he whispered. Polo shook his head. They'll still pin it on you. The police'll come asking questions. You think her husband and boys don't see the way you look at her, as if she was the last fucking Coke in the desert? You think Maroño won't say: it had to be that chubby fuck who spends his whole time over at my house? So I'll kill him too, fuck it! fatboy screamed in a violent outburst, the first Polo had ever seen him have. I'll kill them all so the police think it had to do with some other shit! A break-in! Revenge! Or, I know: we'll chop them up into pieces so they think it was the narcos!

In the beginning Polo thought it was just talk, but after that night, one of countless nights they got so wasted on caña they wound up blowing chunks on the stone steps, he realized fatboy actually meant what he said, to the extent that he'd begun to rope Polo in to his plans, without even asking him first. Why did fatboy trust him? Why did he share all that stuff with Polo? Did he really think they were friends? Or was it a setup maybe, a trap so he could tell that faggot Urquiza that Polo did it? What was he even thinking, a little white boy with the cushiest life, sheltered by everyone around him? He didn't work, he didn't study, he didn't lift a finger; he didn't need to make a future for himself because sooner or later his grandparents would buy him one, no expense spared. Why would someone like that risk throwing everything down the drain just to poke some skanky bitch and confess his undying love to her? He must be crazy, but mental asylum crazy, and Polo too for not having told him where to go, for having spent endless hours listening to him and laughing at his bullshit like a hypocrite and egging him on just so Polo could carry on drinking for free and avoid having to go home to see Zorayda's ugly mug or her belly, or put up with his mother yapping in his ear. That was his mistake, he'd tell them, yet another mistake in a fucking lifetime full of them: believing that it was all just a joke, just talk, and not having got the fuck out of there or refused to meet Franco again the moment the fat fuck got his hands on the gun.

It was his grandfather's, apparently: a solid black piece, a Glock 19, fatboy had said, 'sick'. His granddad was big into firearms; he also had a revolver, but Franco preferred the Glock because it was more accurate, lighter too. Let's have a look, Polo said when fatboy pulled it out. He wanted to touch it to see if it was real; he'd have sworn it was a toy, a matte plastic toy gun; Polo was convinced the dumb fuck was full of shit and that if he pulled the trigger out would pop a lighter flame or a squirt of water. But Franco pretended not to hear him, so Polo couldn't get a good look; it was dark on the steps and the gun was just a shadow in Franco's stubby, pale tamale hands. The next thing, the prick was trying to spin it on his forefinger like the cowboys in the movies, but he fucked it up and the gun slipped off and fell onto the mucara stone steps. Watch it, dickhead, Polo shouted, jumping up from the step where he was sitting. Fatboy burst out laughing. It's not loaded, fool, he drawled as he leant down to pick it up. And if it fires, dickhead? Polo grumbled from five feet away. Calm down, look, it's not loaded, fatboy said, pulling on the slide and producing several clicks to show him that the chamber was empty, but Polo was too far away to see. I'll raid my granddad's bullet supply so we can try it out. The other day he took me to a waste ground near the beach and we were shooting bottles for hours. It's fucking difficult from a distance, but easy enough at close range. He cleared his throat nervously and then wiped his drool with the back of the hand holding the gun.

Polo edged towards him. He still suspected the whole thing was a joke, that the gun was fake and fatboy was just taking him for a ride. He couldn't imagine Franco's grandfather – a rancid, stooped old man, skinny as a rake and with thin grey hair gelled to his skull – firing a gun, it was laughable. He seemed more the kind to collect stamps, or worthless old banknotes, or dead butterflies pinned to pieces of card, anything but knives and guns.

Let's see, he asked fatboy again, holding out his hand. Fatboy smiled and aimed the gun at Polo's head. Don't point that thing at me, asshole! he shouted. You're scared, aren't you? Franco sniggered. You're scared of my gun? I'm scared of your fucking retardedness, Polo muttered with his hands still in the air. Eventually fatboy caved, stood up from the step and, taking the gun by the barrel, offered Polo the grip. It hardly weighed a thing. In the darkness of the mangrove, surrounded by the febrile chorus of the mangrove creepie-crawlies, he felt a sudden urge to be silly: he held the gun in both hands, like the police in the movies, aimed it at fatboy's gut and pulled the trigger. BANG! he shouted, but fatboy didn't move from the spot. Don't fire blanks, you idiot, he grumbled, you'll break it. Is it loud? Polo asked. Franco shrugged his shoulders, or so it seemed in the fading light. Not too loud, he said. Not too loud? What are you talking about, not too loud? Are you fucking kidding me? We can cover it with a pillow, fatboy suggested, like a silencer, or one of those kitchen glove thingies. I read about it online. Bullshit, Polo replied, and he pulled the trigger again. BANG! Take that, you fat motherfucker, you fucking asshole, die, motherfucker, die. Alright, that's enough, pass it here, said fatboy, you're getting jumpy. Bullshit, Polo replied with a great satisfied smile suspended across his face, but in the end, he handed the gun back to Franco. He didn't notice his hands were trembling until he lifted the carton of caña to his mouth. He lit a cigarette and flicked some non-existent ash to hide his agitation. Fatboy carefully squeezed the barrel into the tight waistband of his shorts. You feel like king of the fucking world carrying this thing on you, he sighed. I hope you shoot your balls off, Polo replied, and he burst out laughing. For the first time ever, he felt like he could tell Franco what he really thought, and it was truly liberating. Fatboy looked at him strangely, but seconds later he was also in stitches, unable to contain that high-pitched, ridiculous laugh of his, which provoked even more hilarity in Polo, and soon the pair of them were stretched out on the leaf-mouldy steps, their hysterical laughter ricocheting off the ruin's filthy walls.

It's easy, fatboy said, when at last they calmed down. We slip into the house and jump Moroño, gag him, then find the kids and gag them, and force her to strip. What the fuck do I care if she's dressed or not? Polo said, although a part of him was curious to see Señora Marián naked, just out of interest, nothing morbid. Fine, whatever, I'll take care of that, and in the meantime you can raid the place, fatboy went on. Polo didn't reply. Instead he carried on drinking until he could barely taste the pungent caña or hear the murmuring rain or the rustles coming from the mansion behind them – lizards slinking through the undergrowth, probably, or maybe a crab, rattled by the full moon – and the only sound he could really make out was fatboy, speaking in whispers almost, as if he were afraid someone might hear them in the middle of that jungle, and out of nowhere Polo thought to himself: Why not? Why the fuck not? Nothing made much sense anymore, he really couldn't give a fuck. At the end of the day, why should he care what happened to that slut and her unbearable family, a bunch of smug pricks who thought the world revolved around them. Maybe this was his chance to fuck off out of Progreso and away from his mother's house, away from Zorayda's claws and that shitty job that was a constant, thankless uphill struggle. Fatboy would do it all; fatboy knew the movements of that household, of the boys and even Griselda, the maid who went home to Progreso each Sunday and returned first thing on Monday. Fatboy knew they'd have to sneak in late at night, once the family was already in bed, enter through the kitchen door that those suckers always left open, threaten them and tie them up, at which point Polo would leave fatboy to his filthy shit before they both grabbed as much as they could; the important thing was to make it look like the work of thieves, professional, cold-blooded thieves. They'd throw everything in the back of Señora Marián's SUV and leave the development by the residents' exit, which opened automatically. No one would see who was driving if they wore balaclavas, and in fact, if they hurried up and did it that week, that very Sunday, there'd be no issue at all with security because it was Rosalío's turn to work nights and the guy was a work-dodger, he didn't give a fuck about anything and he'd be asleep without fail by midnight.

Polo hardly slept at all over the following nights, despite his crushing tiredness, despite even the half litre of caña that he and Franco now drank on a daily basis in the zaguan of the abandoned mansion. He'd have liked to sleep for two days straight, but every time he dragged his bones onto the petate, his heart would start racing and his thoughts would spiral out of control, black and deafening and so disjointed that it took him hours to piece them together: that bitch's jewellery, the husband's watches, the games consoles and TVs that, according to fatboy, were all over the house; the white Grand Cherokee, the solitary guard hut in the dead of the night, the pointless ornamental dock, the fig tree's thick, undulating branches, the black river flowing on, indifferent to everything, the lights from the bridge shimmering on the water's surface, Milton's pasty face and sunken eyes, his smile at seeing him in that dazzling snow-white SUV. But at no point, not for a single second – he would tell them

– never in a million years did he imagine hurting the Maroño family. He had nothing against them personally and zero intention of killing or raping anyone; that was all the other guy, that was obsessed fucking fatboy's plan. No one could pin anything other than robbery on Polo, and when they came asking questions, he'd tell them the truth: that it was all fatboy's fault, it was all because of him and the yearning that literally ate away at his brain, he could go fuck himself. His family had the money to shake off the detectives, to smuggle the kid abroad if it came to that and buy the silence of half of Mexico, advantages Polo lacked. If his mother ever found out, she'd probably hand him over herself, which is why he had to get his shit together, keep a clear head, leave nothing to chance and, above all, not trust fatboy's plan. If things went badly, if shit got heavy, he had to be ready to cut and run like the wind out of the development, taking the back route via the dock, or diving headfirst into the river if necessary. How long would it take him to swim to the other side? Twenty minutes, maybe? Half an hour? It'd been months since he'd done it, months since he'd dived into the river to cool down. It couldn't have been more than eighty or ninety yards to the opposite bank, although you had to keep in mind how treacherous the current tended to be at that point, just before the bend that led out into the estuary's open waters. You couldn't trust the deceptive stillness that reigned over the river's surface, much less during the rainy season, when even the henchest motherfucker could drown if he was unlucky enough to get caught up in the branches of a tree being pulled along by the current, especially if he went in alone, and at night, dogged by guilt, but what guilt? Polo wasn't planning on killing anyone, he wasn't planning on using any violence at all; he would just throw what he could into the SUV and give it all to Milton in return for his help. He'd take him the Grand Cherokee and everything in it, even hand over fatboy if it helped; Franco's family was loaded and *they* could demand a healthy ransom for him; and there were no strings attached, Polo didn't want any kind of pay or credit, his cousin could keep the profits, truly, he didn't care. The only thing Polo wanted from his cousin, practically his flesh and blood, was a foot in the door, and Polo knew he wouldn't be able to refuse, that stuff always got to Milton. Polo wasn't asking for much, was he? He just wanted Milton to help him out, just for a while, that's why Polo had to talk to him, to explain that he had no burning ambition to be a squeaker, or a falcon, or an assassin, or to have any other role in the organization; he didn't want to be anyone's bitch, but he was prepared to break his balls working for a while if it meant escaping the rattrap that had been his life since his grandfather died, that was all. He'd work out how to get out of there, where to go, something would come to him later, once it was all over and fatboy had done what he needed to do, if the little faggot even went through with it and didn't chicken out, but Polo didn't want to think too hard about that, about the woman and the kids and that smug bald dick who treated Polo as if he was invisible, unless he wanted Polo to pick up the shit his dogs left at his front door. Polo didn't want to think about that family or imagine any of what was going to happen, he only wanted to focus on the look of surprise on Milton's face when Polo stepped out of the Grand Cherokee and handed him the keys, which is why he spent days trying to call his cousin on the private number he'd given him the last time they'd spoken; and when Milton started sending him straight to voicemail, Polo used up his credit on texts instead, begging his cousin to call him back, which he finally did that Friday at midday, when Polo least expected it, squatting in a ridiculous position in the middle of the extensive lawn that separated the Paradais gardens from the swimming pool area, his eyes locked on a stupid dirt mound a diligent gopher had dug up that morning, scuffing away at the impeccable blanket of lush green grass. Less than ten feet to his right was a second hole in which you could make out the paw prints of the profanatory beast, which Urquiza had ordered him to exterminate, showing no mercy. True to form, his manager had come up with a crackbrained plan, which his subordinate had no choice but to put into action. The fucking imbecile wanted Polo to flood the gopher's burrow: Polo was supposed to push a flowing hose into one of the mounds and then wait next to the other one, machete in hand, ready to pounce on the disgusting vermin when it came running out of its flooded burrow. Polo was so tired he hadn't even bothered trying to tell Urquiza that his plan wouldn't work for shit: every single night, a torrent rained down on that lawn; the gophers were used to it, and in fact, they loved the sludge. The only thing that'd wipe them out was a good dose of rat poison, but Polo also knew Urquiza would reject that idea flat out: all hell would break loose if one of the residents' pets ended up dead or poisoned. No, Polo's best option was to keep his mouth shut, save his breath and go along with his boss's plan, as moronic as it was. And so there he was, sweating his balls off under the scorching July sun, crouched before a mound of freshly dug black earth, his cap on backwards and his machete raised – an agrarian samurai poised to attack, or more like a ridiculous cartoon villain heading for a whopping great fall – when suddenly he felt his phone vibrating in his pocket. He put the machete down to look at the screen. Unknown number. It had to be Milton. ¡What's new, *papi*, what you sayin'! came the cheerful voice of his cousin down the line. He couldn't talk for long, he told him, he had a spare minute so he thought he'd call his bro; he'd seen his texts but hadn't had a chance to reply, they were working him to the bone and shit was pretty fucked up, as Polo could imagine, you had to stick your neck out in that line of work, knuckle down, earn *their* trust, whatever, he didn't have much choice now, nervous laughter and in the background muffled sounds coming from a radio. Polo had stood up and was walking distractedly around the lawn, his phone pressed against his ear so he didn't miss a word, staring at the exquisite grass, as he drifted obliviously towards the development's main street, the machete and hose forgotten by the gopher mound. His cousin was rambling incoherently, and at one point Polo thought he was about to hang up so he jumped in; he really, really needed his help, more than ever, he couldn't stay in Progreso, or in that job where they treated him like a slave, cuz, some stuff had happened at home, some shit with Zorayda, he couldn't go into it now, he wouldn't know where to start, but he wanted Milton to introduce him to *them*, to recommend him, as buddies, man, as *brothers*, Milton, he swore to God he wouldn't pussy out, he swore on his grandfather's grave he had the balls to do whatever they told him to do, anything they wanted; he wasn't the same skinny runt he'd been the last time they saw each other, he'd lost the girly arms Milton had always teased him about; he'd buffed up from sweating his balls off at the development, he could even do heavy lifting, whatever Milton asked, but he needed help, it was a matter of life or death, and Polo went on and on begging like that until Milton cut him off with an irritated sigh and said: *papi*, we've been through this before, I can't, please, don't ask me again, and Polo rolled his eyes while that fucking hypocrite rolled off the same sermon as the last time, about honourable work, about not being anybody's pawn, and about how that job made him wish he was dead. There was a brief silence, abruptly broken by the sound of static and his cousin mumbling something away from his mouthpiece, presumably into a radio, and Polo felt like hurling his phone at the cobbled street and smashing it to pieces, but then Milton came back on the line: Polo, he sighed, and he never called him that – it was always *papi* – give me a second, will you? I'll call you right back, okay? And he hung up without waiting for Polo's reply. Polo was left standing on the edge of the lawn, his phone still in his hand and his eyes welling up with tears of humiliating impotence. A white SUV drove past, its passengers indistinguishable behind the tinted windows but for a pale, chubby face pressed against the backseat window: Micky Maroño sticking his tongue out, misting up the glass with his warm breath.

On Saturday morning, Polo woke up before the horrendous alarm clock jingle. A demonic thirst drove him to his feet, as if pulling him by invisible cords. He was itching for a beer, a beer or three, but he didn't have a peso to his name, so he feigned interest in his mother's morning spiel to see if he could get some money off her, for lunch he'd say, even a fifty. Zorayda had a doctor's appointment that morning, his mother said, stirring sugar into her coffee with an enamel spoon. She'd make the most of her day off to take the girl to the clinic, and maybe they'd finally find out the baby's sex. Zorayda was nibbling at a rock-hard empanada and smiling beatifically, her hand resting on her enormous gut. What the fuck was she so happy about these days? Why did she spend all fucking day rubbing her belly and smiling, especially when she was near Polo? She no longer searched him out when they were alone or rubbed past him when they crossed paths in the hallway, or tried to tickle his arms, *this little ant...* It was as if the baby were enough to fill her up now and somehow made those cat eyes shine even brighter, with new levels of confidence, of audacity; and Polo honestly couldn't stand it, which is why he just sat pretending to count the crumbs on the plastic table cloth.

Fatboy didn't visit him that day, and Polo thought, with bitter-sweet relief, that he'd changed his mind. He dicked around in the development until eight o'clock, but the fat fuck never showed his face, not even at his bedroom window. Rosalío was on the night shift and he watched as Polo removed his overalls and got dressed in his own clothes. What? Polo grunted. Like what you see? Rosalío just looked him up and down and smoothed his wonky moustache. What do you say, kid? One for the road? he proposed. If you're paying, Polo replied, feigning indifference. In any case, drinking with that miserable fart was better than going home and overhearing things he didn't want to know. He cycled down to the store with a couple of empty caguama bottles in his rucksack, paid the clerk for the beers with the banknote Rosalío had given him and walked out into the street, but before getting back on his bike, he changed his mind and went back in to buy a quarter of caña with Rosalío's change and the handful of coins he'd managed to squeeze out of his mother. At the till, the guy from before, the one who always served him, a lanky giant with dandruff, had gone, and in his place was the fat cow with curly hair who was always stirring shit up. Grudgingly he asked her for the quarter of caña but she refused to sell it to him unless he showed her his ID. Polo felt like showing that bitch what he thought of her and tearing the sweets display off the counter onto the floor, but he managed to contain himself and even feign a snarky smile, which was just as well, because as he walked out he came upon a truck packed full of marines in full face coverings heading for the store carpark. Clenching his ass, he cycled away, drenched in the red and blue glow of the roof-mounted lightbar, those flashing lights that seemed to wail *Danger, keep your shit together*. Of course, the caguamas didn't last two minutes in the sweltering security hut. Rosalío, like a good drunk, started regaling his life story to Polo after just a few drinks, his voice gravelly from the booze. The old man went on and on, interspersing his incoherent monologue with silences and throat-clears as if to imbue the few comprehensible words he garbled with meaning, before eventually he fell asleep with his head resting on his folded arms against the back of the chair he was straddling. Polo took his chance to watch the screen displaying a mosaic of images captured by Paradais's numerous security cameras. Maybe no one had cleaned the lenses for a long time, or maybe the resolution was just poor and in black and white, because not once could Polo make out the faces of the residents who pulled up before the automatic boom barrier and waited for it to be raised. That fat fuck had been right.

When he got home, he was surprised to find his mother still awake, watching a film on the TV positioned on the chest of drawers in front of the bed. She had the volume turned down low so as not to wake Zorayda, who was sleeping peacefully curled up in the adjacent bed, the one that had been Polo's before she took it from him. The air from the fan was ruffling his cousin's loose hair and if it hadn't been for the immense bulge of her belly stretching the threadbare t-shirt she used for pyjamas, Polo might have believed that that mellow young woman sucking her thumb in her sleep was the same twelve-year-old-girl he'd met during that damn trip to Mina. His mother, propped up by a couple of big pillows and her hair still damp from her evening wash, was eating peanuts from an enormous bag resting on her belly; the bag rustled every time she moved her hand in or out of it, but the noise didn't wake Zorayda. He watched them both for a long time from the darkness of the threshold, until his mother noticed him with a start and, instead of calling him a shit or asking where the fuck he'd been all evening like normal, invited him to join her in the bedroom, like the old times when they would watch TV together in the evenings, side by side but each in their own bed. Polo hesitated for a moment before going in and perching on the edge of his mother's mattress, far away enough from the fan to avoid offending her with his unholy stench of sweat and rancid beer. There was a love scene on the TV: in what looked like a girl's bedroom, a slim young man with blond hair and markedly European looks was kissing another light-skinned young woman with brown hair set in curls, while in the background a guitar played and a bodiless voice crooned away about the different emotions a man goes through when he first sets eyes on his future lover, comparing the feeling to a glorious sunrise in a grey wilderness, to the flutter of butterfly wings laced with pearls, even to an earthquake. Then, the singer's voice faded to make way for the couple's sweet nothings, whispered between caresses until the untimely appearance of an older man with thick sideburns in the doorway. The couple jumped apart and the blond boy was chastised before disappearing from the scene, while the girl, her face streaked with tears, collapsed onto the bed and wept into her strawberry milkshake-coloured pillow. The theme tune, this time without lyrics and played with more downcast and sinister inflections, grew suddenly louder before fading out entirely, cutting to a commercial for sanitary towels. His mother let out a cynical grunt and said something Polo didn't catch, but which gave him an opportunity to get up and turn in for the night. What is it, son? his mother asked him. You tired? Polo nodded. I'm going to sleep. His mother didn't take her eyes off the screen. You do that, she replied with a mouth full of peanuts. In the living room, Polo got undressed and lay down on the old petate steeped in his own bodily fluids, but he barely slept a wink. It didn't rain that night, but an unexpected gale blew in from the coast and spent a good part of the night lashing against the windows and doors, rattling them in their frames and making Polo think someone was trying to break in: his grandfather, risen from the tomb, he thought incoherently, just before sunrise. By the time his mother's phone alarm went off, he felt like he'd only slept for half an hour. He stretched out on the petate and ran through a checklist of complaints: he had a headache, a sore throat, tender feet and knees, he felt slightly sick and a morbid lethargy was pinning him to the floor. Only his mother could snap him out of it: you'll be late again, you lazy slob! Who the hell do you think you are?

He spent all of Sunday morning in a filthy mood. At lunchtime he rode down to the store, bought himself a Coke and drank it under the sign forbidding the consumption of alcoholic drinks. He watched car after car park up, their passengers dressed in swimming suits, stopping off at the store on their way to the beach to buy snacks and cold drinks: potbellied men in shorts, women wearing ridiculous straw hats that the wind threatened to blow away, and whining kids dragging their buckets and spades and inflatable orcas behind them. It was the perfect day for basking in the sun; maybe that's why it came as no surprise to find fatboy lounging on one of the sunbeds around the pool, dressed in the same swimming trunks he'd worn the first day they'd drunk together on the dock, towards the end of the party for that little freak Micky Maroño who, incidentally, was also there that day, thrashing around in the kids' pool with two other brats from the development, under the harried gaze of the uniformed maid. Polo walked over casually and began to pick up the rubbish that had accumulated around the pool, moving steadily closer to fatboy, who was pretending to doze with his hands crossed beneath his head and whose face was half covered by a pair of giant sunglasses. Even his underarm hair was fair, a brownish-grey colour. Polo clenched his fists at the mere sight of his flabby, greased-up gut, scored with red stretchmarks. He turned away to see Micky walking towards the edge of the main pool – ignoring the maid's panicked orders not to – and then throwing himself in. His tiny frame, slippery and sinewy like the body of a baby crocodile, glided through the water, almost to the bottom, and was down there for a long time until at last he came up, his eyes bulging, his little arms flapping about and a big toothy smile plastered across his face, to the obvious relief of the maid who had been about to dive in to rescue the little brat and was now standing with one brown hand on her trembling chest. A slap on the wrist, the boy's derisive laughter, the white, washed-out sky hazy under the sun's ferocious heat, the water clear and blue like no other water Polo had ever seen. He felt an overwhelming urge to plunge into that pool before the horrified eyes of the maid and those unbearable snot-nosed kids; an urge to escape the heat; to dive, like the boy, to the bottom of that crystal clear water, right down until his stomach grazed the elegant blue mosaic floor, not the muddy, mulchy riverbed of the Jamapa, the only 'pool' Polo had ever known. An unsettling breeze blew in from the river, carrying the scent of lime, and fatboy, now beside Polo, seemed to snap out of his daydream. Who knew what he'd been thinking about, but now he was smiling. Polo pretended to clean up the cigarette butts next to his sunbed. All set? fatboy asked. His voice sounded croaky, out of sorts. What happened to you? Polo asked him, spotting the pinkish-purplish bruise peeping out from behind Franco's sunglasses on his left eye. Franco's smile froze and then grew wider; wider and deader. My dad paid us a visit, he said, and my grandparents told him all about my antics. So he punished you? Polo asked, but fatboy just shrugged his shoulders and uncrossed his hands; one of his fingers, his right middle one, was in a strapping. At nine then? he asked Polo. You sure they'll lend you the car? Polo replied. Fatboy put his hand in the pocket of his trunks and pulled out the keys to his grandparents' Honda. Polo walked away with the rubbish bag in his hand and his heart pounding in his chest.

The rain started just after seven, a sudden and deafening downpour that forced Polo to take refuge in Rosalío's hut. The guard had his lips wrapped around an unlabelled bottle of sweet anis. Polo removed his overalls and put on his own clothes. Have a sip, kid, Rosalío said. You leaving already? Urquiza told me to tell you to mop the pool area. Is he fucking kidding, it's raining! No one's even by the pool now, Polo protested. Rosalío looked at him, taken aback. What's the hurry, kid? Is there a little piece of ass you're creaming your pants to see waiting for you somewhere? A dumb chuckle, the oversweet stench of moonshine on his breath. Polo grabbed the bottle and took a swig. That stuff was so cheap, so toxic it made his throat burn and clamp up. Jesus fucking Christ, he spluttered. How can you drink this shit? Oh, very fine tastes, Rosalío sniggered. The rain fell heavier. From the security hut window you could barely make out the houses in the development; fatboy's, for example, had disappeared behind a greyish curtain. Rosalío groped the wall until he found the light switch. Have a proper drink, kid, while we wait for it to stop, he proposed, but Polo turned down the offer. Better if the old man drank that shit himself so that by the early hours he'd be well and truly gone, dead to the world in his grubby plastic seat. Polo stayed there a little longer, twenty or so minutes that felt like an eternity, half listening to Rosalío's drunken blathering and half trying to figure out when the rain would stop, until finally it did let up enough for him to leave the hut without looking like a total weirdo. He grabbed his bike, but instead of riding it, he pushed it along by the handlebars and headed onto the neighbouring property making absolutely sure not to be seen. He walked until he reached the abandoned mansion, where he hid his bike in a corner of the zaguan. By then the storm had petered out to a drizzle and fat raindrops dripped from the overcrowded canopy above. He smoked a couple of cigarettes standing up so as not to get a wet ass from the steps. Pacing around in circles he sang under his breath, *voy a llenarte toda toda*, the first crap that came into his head, *lentamente y poco a poco*, over and over so he didn't have to think about the rustles coming from the house, *con mis besos*, or the ghostly eyes he felt sure were spying on him from the murky depths of that building. When his phone showed nine on the dot, he cut across the mansion plot and came out onto the street where Franco was waiting for him at the wheel of his grandparents' car. Don't get the seats dirty. If those two find a single mark they will fuck me so hard, was the first thing the tubster said. Polo's mind wandered to the image of fatboy's massive coiffed grandmother riding the pale, podgy body of her grandson, butt naked, her rosy breasts juddering up and down, like two saggy sacks, while the bag-of-bones grandfather watched with his head bent down, feebly tugging away as his pecker, and Polo stuck out his tongue in disgust. Fatboy was a good driver, confident, but even so, Polo couldn't help holding onto his seat and grabbing the handle above his head. The rain had stopped but every few seconds a bolt of lightning would rip a line through the black, swollen sky. By that point it was completely dark outside, but that fat twat Franco was still wearing his sunglasses. Polo was about to tell him to take them off – he wanted to see the shiner his father had given him, for answering him back, probably – but he decided it wasn't the right moment. Franco could do what he liked. Polo didn't open his mouth again until they were in the DIY section of Walmart, where they had to decide what to use to tie up and gag the Maroños. Fatso had already tossed four packets of brown packing tape into the trolley, along with two torches and spare batteries, two pairs of black trousers – medium for Polo and extra-large for fatboy – two hoodies – also black – and finally two packs of the darkest women's tights they could find, because at that time of year they didn't stock either the balaclavas or gloves the pair had planned to buy. Polo was sure that wasn't the right tape. That's not it, you prick, he hissed. What the fuck are you talking about? fatboy replied. I'm telling you it's not what we need. It has to have threads in it, dickhead! What fucking threads, you idiot? Threads my fucking ass! Can I help you, gentlemen? came a nasal little voice from behind them. It was a girl, a teenager like them, wearing an enormous orange vest and thick black-rimmed glasses. We're looking for that grey tape... Polo muttered. Grey tape? she repeated. Her yellow teeth, covered in train tracks and elastics, were making him nervous. Yeah, that grey tape that's sort of got thread running through it, he managed to explain. Oh! exclaimed the girl, you're looking for kidnapper tape! and she bent down to look around on the bottom shelf. Fatboy started giggling hysterically and Polo had to elbow him and step on his foot. That's what people call it, the girl said with her metal smile. They had to wait for her to walk away before throwing four more rolls of duct tape into the trolley and making their way over to the checkouts. Fatboy, still wearing his sunglasses, dumped their purchases onto the conveyor belt, finally adding two boxes of condoms that he took from the shelf next to the magazines and chocolate bars. Almost forgot, he said with a wink, and Polo felt his stomach turn. He watched their items glide through the checkout and for a moment he was convinced that the cashier, a woman with coppery-purplish hair and deep wrinkles, would call the police when she saw what they were buying; it was so obvious what they wanted all that for. Fucking fatboy was such a stupid prick, and Polo an even bigger prick for having listened to him. The police would be outside waiting for them when they walked out of there; he almost thought he could hear the sirens wailing in the near distance. And even then that retard, that fat fuck tried to strike up small talk with the cashier: crazy rain, eh, how about the street floods, terrible leaks in the store; it was like he was trying to make the woman remember them. Polo pulled his cap right down over his eyebrows; he didn't know where to put his hands, whether to let them hang by his sides, fold them, or put them in his pockets. He looked around and noticed CCTV cameras all over the place and he couldn't understand why fatboy was taking so long to pay and get the fuck out of there. He felt a stabbing pain in his bladder but couldn't tell if he needed to pee or if it was simply the frozen weight of panic.

The supermarket was full of bad-tempered customers, annoyed about having to do their weekly shopping on a Sunday night. On the plus side, the checkout lady seemed particularly tired and fed up after hours on her feet, serving assholes by the bulk, and she barely muttered monosyllabic replies to fatboy's chirpy banter. She didn't even look up when it came to handing over their change and receipt because it was already time to start scanning the next poor bastard's items. When they finally left the supermarket, Polo stopped to pick up the receipt fatboy had scrunched into a ball and thrown on the ground by the exit. It's evidence, you retard, he said. Fatboy scoffed when he saw Polo unfold the receipt in his hands and tear it up into tiny pieces, which he held in his clenched fist until he could throw them out of the moving car as they crossed the bridge.

The plan was for Polo to enter the development unseen, inside the boot of the car, and for him to remain hidden in the Andrades' garage until fatboy came to get him at three in the morning, the time they'd agreed to head over to the Maroños' house. Polo was less than pleased about fatboy's hiding place: a tiny bathroom, the width of a hallway and with such a low ceiling Polo could barely stand up, with an unusable shower and toilet buried under a barricade of boxes, piles of old magazines, paint cans and a staggering array of junk, including a huge bag of golf clubs and a standing fan. The pair argued in whispers for about a minute until fatboy eventually shoved Polo inside. Get some sleep, he hissed, before locking the door. Polo felt like screaming loud enough to wake up the whole house, but instead he moved some stuff around to make space for himself and sat down, hugging his knees to his chest and resting his head on his forearms. He couldn't sleep, but nor did he dare go over the plan again; his mind kept wandering. Was he really going to go through with it? Was he really as crazy as fucking fatboy? Crazy enough to go through with that stupid, ridiculous, childish idea? And all so Franco could dip his wick in some woman! As if a rotten swamp of a cunt justified all that effort, all that energy, the carnage that was to come, their lives devastated, everything gone for a second-rate fucking snatch: a grubby, slimy, murky hole. What was that fat fucker even thinking? And what if he changed his mind at the last minute? What if the woman got down on her knees and begged the kid for mercy? And what if he couldn't shoot them? What if the shots woke the neighbours? Franco would be in the juvie courts before he knew it. Or maybe not, maybe his grandparents or his bent lawyer father could save him, but Polo, who had just turned sixteen that February, would be packed off with the big boys if that selfish prick Milton refused to help him out, or if Polo didn't make it out of the development after the showdown, either way. He was dying for a drink. He was absolutely dying of thirst but Franco had refused to buy any booze at the supermarket because, according to him, they needed clear heads, or some bullshit; more like fatboy was scared it'd keep him from getting it up when the time came, and he was probably rubbing one out in his room right now while Polo sweated his balls off in that stuffy hole where he couldn't even take a leak for fear of waking up the house. He thought about pissing against the sink anyway, soaking the magazines piled up against the porcelain; he thought about forcing the lock on the door and getting the hell out of there, aborting their ridiculous plan, but eventually he did fall asleep, and so deeply that he didn't even hear Franco open the door and whisper his name: Polo, Polo wake up, dickhead! For a moment, Polo thought it was his mother speaking, his mother slapping him and pulling at his clothes to get him up and off to school, to send him job hunting in Boca, or to go and water the sempiternal lawns of Paradais, and he wanted to turn over on his petate and carry on sleeping, but just then he hit his head against the golf bag and the chinking of the metal clubs finally brought him around. It's time, asshole, Franco muttered, and he started to undress right there in the garage. His skin gleamed, pale but rosy, and almost completely hairless, like a pig's skin after the slaughter, all red and with hair only on the groin and balls. He wasn't wearing his sunglasses now and his left eye was still swollen and bruised, as was his right middle finger, which he removed from its strapping with a wince before pulling on his hoodie; even the extra-large fit him snuggly, and his torso looked like a poorly wrapped tamale. Polo struggled to his feet, his entire body aching and tingly. I need a piss, he told Franco. Well, you'll have to hold it in, he replied. First things first, and Franco got down on one knee and tied the strap of a sheath around his right calf; he still hadn't put on his trousers and his drooping penis was dangling down, tapered at the tip and shrivelled, disgusting, Polo thought. Poking out from the sheath was the wooden handle of a huge knife with a long blade, almost black in colour, which looked ancient, like something from the stone age. What the fuck is that? he asked fatboy. A combat knife, replied the idiot. Did you steal that, too? No, he said, pulling up his trousers and checking the time. It's mine, my grandfather gave it to me. It was his father's, from when he fought in the war. Polo was about to ask which war he was talking about, when suddenly he felt a rumbling, gurgling sensation in his guts; not only was he about to piss himself, but he felt he might actually shit himself from nerves too. He clenched his sphincter muscles as he got changed. Ready? fatboy

112

asked. He seemed calm but the son of a bitch's voice was quaking. And your piece? Polo asked in reply. Fatboy pointed at his trouser fly. The Glock, dickhead, Polo said, giving him the middle finger. Franco let out a horrible screeching laugh, like the sound of a saw cutting through iron. The gun was in the front pocket of his hoodie, duly loaded, he explained. They pulled the tights over their heads. It was a horrible, suffocating feeling. They looked so ridiculous they almost got the giggles when they saw each other. They hadn't managed to find any normal gloves in the supermarket, so they had to make do with the surgical kind, which made their palms sweat. They shoved their clothes inside a rubbish bag and dumped that in the bin beside the garage door on their way out.

What happened next, between the hours of three and seven on that Monday morning in late July, Polo would recall as a series of independent, almost soundless instants: the freezing rain falling in heavy, plump drops onto their masked faces; the urge to pee confused with fear as they snuck in through the kitchen door, which, just as fatboy had predicted, was neither locked nor bolted; the sheer amount of furniture inside that house: armchairs, side tables, easy chairs, shelves and lamps that filled the huge living room, which was lit by a strip of cold light built into a false ceiling; the cream rug on the floor; the coolness of the air con, which immediately made his nose and chest stuffy; the look of horror on Andy's face as he sat up in bed after they opened the door to his bedroom on the ground floor beside the staircase; the way his bony body wriggled under their combined weight as they pinned him down on the bed; the difficulty of getting the grey tape onto his skin and of keeping the ends from sticking together as they tied the kid's strong legs, as they twisted his smooth child's arms behind his back and prised open his jaw to stuff a pillowcase into his mouth amid his breathless sobs; the walk upstairs in the pitch darkness; the half-open door to the other boy's room, crammed full of toys like some kind of Christmas fantasy, the empty bed, the bedsheets thrown to the floor; Maroño creeping out onto the landing, his horrified expression on seeing them, his hands raised in front of his face, the bedroom light still on; the door slamming after a brief struggle; the barrel of the gun level with Polo's face, pointing the other way; Señora Marián awake, sitting on the edge of the bed, the child Micky in her arms, his face buried in her chest; Maroño shielding them both with his body, his arms outstretched in a peace-making gesture; *take everything*, he was saying, in the moments Polo could hear him, while he taped up the man's hands and ankles, *take everything, I'll give you the keys, the code to the safe, whatever you want, but please,* all to the sound of the woman's sobs and the little boy's yelps and Franco's hysterical outbursts, his calls for silence: *shut up, shut up the lot of you, I can't hear myself think, for fuck's sake,* as if he didn't know what came next, what the next step was, and the truth was Polo couldn't remember either; *the boy, take the boy,* fatboy said suddenly, *take him downstairs to his brother, he can't know*; the woman's eyes like saucers as she recognized them both, even with the tights covering their faces; how tightly she clung to the boy in her arms, refusing to hand him over, impervious to the gun; the surprising sweetness with which Polo then addressed her: *don't worry, Señora, I'll look after him, I'll take him to his brother, I promise*; the woman's trembling, suddenly empty hands; her pale, faintly lined mouth; the slack, freckled skin of her breasts peeping out from the plunging neckline of her satin nightie; the loud bang of the gunshot to Maroño's head, the shot that shook the room, the whole house, the wet street, and surely the whole development and all the way in Boca del Río, as Maroño's body collapsed onto the bedside table, a bloody hole blossoming in the socket of his blasted eye; the strangulated scream Señora Marián let out before fatboy threatened her into silence with the gun; the boy thrashing around in Polo's arms, kicking him in the shins with his tiny bare feet; fatboy delicately closing the bedroom door; Micky's sudden docility the moment he was left alone with Polo in the darkness of the landing; the struggle to get back to Andy's room; the teenager's skinny body writhing on the floor, his back arched and his chest heaving from the effort of breathing through his inflamed nostrils, the only part the tape didn't cover; the trickle of snot from Micky's nose that Polo had to wipe away with a dirty sock before kneeling down in front of the boy and taping up his hands; the glint of terror in the boy's green, marbly eyes when Polo asked him to open his mouth and bite down hard on the sock, now tied in a knot; fatboy's voice in his head – *take the boy, take him downstairs, do the same as we did to his brother, they can't know* – as he wrapped that mouth in layer upon layer of tape and Micky's eyes filled with tears, his nose streaming again; then repeating it all with Andy, covering his entire face with tape, leaving not an inch of rosy skin exposed: *they can't know*; the overwhelming urge to drink that came over Polo when he finished his job with the boys and went back into the hallway, closing the door behind him; the look of distress on fatboy's face, no longer hidden under the tights, when Polo finally plucked up the courage – after downing half a bottle of tequila blanco taken from Maroño's fully stocked bar – to go upstairs and ask him what the next phase of the plan was because he'd forgotten; Señora Marián's pendulous breasts and brown nipples joggling like udders as she wept, curled up in a

115

corner of the bedroom, dressed only in a pair of pink panties; Maroño's legs poking out from the duvet now covering his body on the floor on the other side of the bed, the bloodstain on the white fabric expanding as a furious fatboy tramped about the room keeping his eyes locked on the cowering woman and shouting, *help me tie her up, this is harder than I thought, she won't let me do anything*, his left hand tugging away at his dick to save his mediocre erection and his right hand wielding the gun; the faint whisper of a voice that spoke to Polo as he taped together Señora Marián's wrists: *Polo, help us, you don't have to do this, Polo, I know you're a good man, help us, please*, before Polo knelt down on one knee to tie her ankles too; the jab in the ribs from an indignant Franco: *I told you just the hands, for fuck's sake, how am I supposed to fuck her if you tie her legs together?* as he pulled out the knife strapped to his shin to cut the tape again; fatboy's coos and caresses as he tried to soothe the woman: *it's okay, my love, it's okay, baby, everything's going to be okay, I just want you to suck it for me, alright? Just a little bit*; the walk back downstairs and straight to Maroño's bar for some liquid pain relief after that fat fucker kicked him; his mouth smothering each and every one of the open bottles in kisses; his fumbling search around the house, cherry-picking valuables, all the things he'd dreamed about stealing and which he could no longer care less about: the keys to the white Grand Cherokee, Señora Marián's handbag, the flat screen in the study, the only one he could actually get to the living room because the rest were fixed to the walls, the game consoles, the camera, phone and laptop on the desk in Andy's room, which was glacial from the air conditioning and the dead silence in there, the two boys unmoving on the floor, their backs arched, *they can't know*; his lurching return to the master bedroom; Franco's exasperated cry on hearing his gentle knocks at the door: *what the fuck do you want now! I'm trying to concentrate!*; the argument over the jewels and watches; Franco's angry exhalation before he clambered onto the bed where the woman was now lying; Señora Marián's pleading eyes, which followed Polo to the walk-in wardrobe; the skin on her legs covered in red marks and scratches; Polo's frantic search inside drawers and cabinets; the handbag he emptied to stuff with the jewels and watches he ripped from velvet boxes and pouches, and which he then tucked inside his waistband and covered with his hoodie; the face of a lunatic reflected back at him, fierce and desperate, when he removed the tights from his head and looked in the mirror; fatboy's flat, quivering buttocks as he lay facedown on the bed, his head of blond curls buried between the woman's spread legs while she wept in silence: what was he doing fucking wasting time like that! Why didn't he hurry up and fuck her so they could get out of there?; the sound of the howling wind outside, so like the wailing sirens of the police cars that were surely on their way, alerted by the gunshot, by the Maroños' screams, coming to knock down the door and arrest them any minute now; the blessed return to the home bar, the gentle pecks he placed on Maroño's beautiful bottles; the sudden realization that he had to piss immediately or his bladder would burst; the shiver that coursed through him, all the way down to his bones, when at last he relieved himself, loudly, in the air-freshened bathroom next to the walk-in wardrobe; the sense of dread when he looked at his phone and saw the time; the wave of tiredness that came over him on remembering that he still had to get his spoils into the white Grand Cherokee; the sudden fear that fatboy would decide to pop a cap in him too once he'd finished; tripping and falling onto the plush carpet on his way to perk himself up with another few swigs; the effort to get up and haul the stolen goods to the garage and into the SUV, and the rage he felt on realizing that he was crying, that big fat teardrops were running down his cheeks and kept on coming even when he slapped them away; the terrible, animal cry, or rather roar, that broke the dead silence of Polo's panic; the stumbling race down the hallway; the awful vision of the naked woman at the top of the stairs, that prehistoric knife in her hand, her tits and face covered in blood, her demented eyes bearing down on him; the stream of liquid faeces that escaped Polo's anus on remembering the legend, the Bloody Countess coming to get him; the shot that rang out from the stairwell and which sent the witch tumbling head over heels to the ground floor; fatboy's sobs as he clung to her body; the woman's death rattle as she choked on the bloodstained carpet; the unbearable weight of fatboy pressing down on Polo's shoulders and back as they made their way to the garage; the wet whistle emanating from Franco's lungs, the blood that gushed from his half-open mouth, ran down his chest and dripped onto the carpet in big black drops; fatboy's fumbling attempts to climb into the SUV; the thud of his forehead against the wheel as he collapsed, the frothing knife wounds on his back, the deep, hissing gashes that Polo hadn't spotted before; the frenzied dance – there was no other way to put it – that possessed him for a few minutes, the pacing back and forth in that garage wondering what to do, then pulling his hair and whimpering when it hit him that fatboy was dead, that they were *all* dead, *they were all dead*, before pulling himself together and deciding that he had to get out of there that minute; and then, the escape via the kitchen door; the cautious dash to the dock in the pouring rain; the Bloody Countess's deranged face peering out at him from behind the fig tree, from the riverbank reeds, at every step, in every shadow; the irresistible urge to dive into the river and the absolute certainty that spectres couldn't get across water; the certain knowledge that he had just committed the worst mistake of his life, this time really the worst fucking mistake of his shitty, miserable life, as he sank like a rock into the water and his cotton clothes turned to lead and his work boots dragged him down to the river-bed and the ruthless current pulled him out to the estuary, towards the bridge where, as a child, he used to fish at his grandfather's side while they talked about the boat they'd one day build together while downing great glugs of the old man's homebrew on the sly; the paralysing dread on realizing that the lights in Progreso – his one indicator to help him reach the other side – were growing more dis-tant, despite his desperate thrashing and kicking; the deadly exhaustion that slowly started to numb his limbs; the rain water that poured into his gasping mouth when he came up for breath; the atrocious sense that there was something tailing him in the water, an enormous, scaly creature that kept sliding between his legs and that, at any moment, would sink its sharp jaws into him; the long, long while – most of the night, it seemed to him – he spent lying face down on a sandy bank, his arms and legs wrapped in thick tangles of water hyacinths, learning to breathe again like a new-born baby; and then the last stretch along the pitch-dark dirt track to the infernal chirping of crickets and cicadas, a deathly racket that em-bedded itself in his skull, together with the eerie wail of persecutory police cars in the distance, which he could still hear in his head long after he'd emerged from the old tunnel and walked into his house through the back door and collapsed, fully dressed, onto the petate laid out on the floor.

He had lost everything: his keys, his shoes, his phone, his bike, his rucksack with his work overalls, and the handbag containing the Maroños' jewels, but it didn't matter because he was alive: he'd crossed the Jamapa in the middle of a storm, in the pitch darkness of that frenzied night, and he had come out the other side purified and redeemed, or so he believed. He closed his eyes and passed out for about an hour, until the damn phone alarm emitted its grim jingle and his mother shuffled out of her room in her flipflops and began shouting at him that it was time to get up, wake up you waste of space, it's always the same with you, why can't you just be responsible for once? Polo tried to get up off the floor but he couldn't: each and every muscle in his body was screaming in pain. His mother sidled over to him. What's wrong with you? she asked, warily. I'm sick, Polo moaned, I can't open my eyes. His eyes were stuck together with a gluey green crust, like that summer as a boy when he'd gone for a long swim in the river and caught conjunctivitis. Sick? his mother grumbled. Drunk, more like, I can smell you from here. You really are a waste of space, this is all I needed, and out of nowhere, catching Polo completely off-guard – because it had been years since his mother last did it – she smacked him across the face with the sole of her flipflop, and then on the back of his neck, and his backside, again and again, screaming madly: who said you could go out on the lash, you son of a bitch, and on a Sunday, you irresponsible shit! You'll get up right now, right this second, do you hear me! Who the hell do you think you are?

He would have liked to tell her the truth: that it wasn't his fault, that it was all fatboy's fault; tell her about Franco's sick obsession with that woman who, as it turned out, would rather die than give herself to him, but it was all Polo could do to get up off the floor, splash his face in the drum in the yard, get dressed in his faded overalls and leave the house – without any breakfast, without so much as a sip of water because his stomach was still in knots – and cycle off on Zorayda's yellow bicycle, his eyes blurry from tiredness and from the nasty green gunk still oozing from them, along the same old road, the road his muscles knew from memory, and which, in that moment, was more arduous than ever, precisely because everything around him seemed so normal. It was all completely unchanged: the bridge arching over the river; the sun shining behind the trees, tender and fragrant after the nocturnal rains; the barbed wire crowning the immense boundary walls of the luxury residential developments, glistening with dew. Even Cenobio, the day guard, greeted him from his post as normal, as if nothing special or strange or terrifying had gone on in Paradais the night before and Rosalío hadn't reported the sound of any gunfire before handing him the keys to the security hut and the record sheet where they wrote down the registration numbers of the visitors' cars.

Even Urquiza was in earlier than usual and ordered Polo to sweep the huge quantities of leaves and broken branches that the storm had thrown at the development's main entrance. From there, with the broom tightly clutched in his trembling hands, Polo watched the parade of luxury cars carrying their residents, sweet-smelling assholes leaving for their offices and dolled-up señoras taking their uniformed kids to school. At a certain point, it occurred to Polo that any moment now he'd see Señora Marián driving by in her white SUV, her hair loose and hanging neatly at her shoulders, her arms covered in jangling bangles and her ruby red lips curled into a come-hither smile, while her two spoiled brats squabbled in the back, and he felt his knees buckle, as if he were about to faint. The broom slipped from his hands when Griselda, the Maroños' maid, hurried past him wearing her immaculate domestic uniform and carrying her travel case, trotting in the direction of house number seven, the only one that still had its security lights on and its curtains drawn, as if it were still night. In that moment, he would tell them, he felt a fleeting temptation to run, to jump onto his cousin's bike and cycle somewhere very far away, it didn't matter where, as far as he could from that place, but there was something stopping him: the comforting certainty of his total innocence. It was all Franco Andrade's fault, Polo had only done what he was told; the poor sucker had lost his mind over that woman, although Polo couldn't see why. And he had genuinely believed it was all just fatboy's idea of a joke, drunk talk to fill the night air with something other than their cigarette smoke; how was he supposed to know fatboy was being serious, when all Polo had ever wanted was to put off going home. He was sick to death of it all, that town, his job, his mother's lectures and his cousin's digs, sick of the life he led, and he wanted to be free, free goddammit, *that* was his life goal, and he'd only just figured it out. Free, whatever it took, he'd tell them, and it would be Polo himself who would raise the barrier to the police cars when they showed up later, with their sirens off but ready, like dogs in pursuit of their prey.

Fitzcarraldo Editions
8-12 Creekside
London, SE8 3DX
United Kingdom

ISBN 978-1913097-87-5

Design by Ray O'Meara
Typeset in Fitzcarraldo
Printed and bound by TJ Books

fitzcarraldoeditions.com

Fitzcarraldo Editions